WOR
LAID PLANS

AN ANTHOLOGY OF VACATION HORROR

FOREWORD BY
SADIE HARTMANN

EDITED BY
SAMANTHA KOLESNIK

GRINDHOUSE
PRESS

Grindhouse Press
PO BOX 521
Dayton, Ohio 45401

Grindhouse Press #068
ISBN-13: 978-1-941918-70-8

TABLE OF CONTENTS

FOREWORD
Sadie Hartmann

My parents planned the same family vacation every year. Sometime in October or November, we packed our bags into the station wagon and traveled a little over three hours from our home in the Sierra Nevada Foothills to the North Coast. On the way to Dillon Beach, we'd often stop in Petaluma for lunch. Late afternoon, we'd get to the beach house, aptly named, Wit's End. This is where we stayed for about a week to ten days every year.

We never complained or whined about going someplace new. Going to Dillon Beach was better than Christmas. The house was always the same. We knew what to expect. My sisters and I planned our activities for every day: beachcombing, viewing tide pools, hiking, shopping, reading, and playing board games. Every year, we created our Best Laid Plans and executed them accordingly based on experience and familiarity.

I'm telling you this because it primes the pump for what I'm going to tell you now, which is:

I'm a creature of habit and I don't like adventure.

I'm the best possible person to introduce you to the stories in this collection because, collectively, they are the Worst Laid Plans. You need to be warned.

It might not be a good idea to vacation somewhere you've never been before. Imagine all the unknown variables! What if you find

I

yourself stranded on the side of the road in a strange place and you have to rely on strangers to help you out? You could be forced to make a hasty decision that could cost valuable vacation time or, more importantly, your very lives! Don't talk to strangers. If it's true for kids, it's true for anyone. Keep to yourself when you're out adventuring; better yet, just stay home!

It's my recommendation that you steer clear of all RV parks. You never know what kind of people have parked their trailer there to watch you through its grimy windows. Besides, there's not much to do at RV parks. I imagine guests get pretty bored, and boredom often leads to unsavory activities. Like they say, idle hands make the devil's work. This goes for camping, too. I can't imagine why anyone would think it's a good idea to drag all of their nice things out into nature and sleep in a tent. There's nothing but a thin layer of fabric to protect you from . . . ANYTHING. Camping is one of the worst laid plans.

I mentioned earlier that my family enjoyed vacationing at the beach. My concern is that you will be inspired to do the same, but let me caution you: not all beaches are created equal! Some beaches attract 'unkindly girls' and that can lead to trouble. Case in point, I heard of a beautiful creature in a bikini that preyed on spring breakers in Cancun, but I don't imagine a monster can stay in one place for long. Reason enough to go to more private beaches.

Wait, scratch that. If you're at an isolated beach, be aware of your surroundings. You never know what might creep out of the ocean and lure you into unsafe waters.

You also might be tempted to trust a tour guide to take you out to sea for an experience you won't soon forget! It's my gut feeling that going out in the middle of the ocean, where nobody can hear you scream, is not the safest option if you love your life. Beach excursions are one of the worst laid plans. You could wind up having to send out an SOS or a message in a bottle. Not ideal.

Sometimes people get excited about seeing some sights! This sounds like a good plan, but I would caution against it. What if you find yourself in a cave with beautiful, natural formations but you have no idea that it's also home to subterranean creatures! It's best to stay above ground and out of harm's way. In fact, I would avoid any of nature's unpredictable locations; you just never know what kind of wildlife you could encounter.

Maybe it would be a good plan to travel to one of any special conventions. There's a convention for just about anything! Books, movies, comics, and more! There's even a convention for people who are passionate about big reptiles. The folks there cosplay as crocodiles and alligators. Seems relatively safe. What could happen?

The same goes for theme parks. I don't think going someplace that touts itself as the happiest place on earth could ever disappoint. I'm pretty sure fairytale princesses are the kindest, safest people you'll ever meet. A solid choice if you have a family or rambunctious twins!

The stories you are about to read are not true. They're fiction. But before you pack your bags and head off to some enticing vacation destination, it's in your best interest to take these stories to heart and make informed decisions about your life choices. It could make the difference between sunning yourself on the beach, getting your tan on, or keeping your skin on at all.

Safe travels!
Sadie Hartmann

WORST LAID PLANS

YOU'VE BEEN SAVED

S.E. Howard

"REMEMBER THE TIME MIKEY BUSTED us into his uncle's house to get that fifth of Jack Daniel's he swore was hidden underneath the kitchen sink?"

Using nothing but his driver's permit, Chris Flynn thought as his friend, Ethan Brooks, said this aloud.

"Using nothing but his goddamn driver's permit, you remember that? He jimmies it between the door and the jamb . . ."

Gives it a wiggle or two to wedge it underneath the bolt . . . Chris thought.

". . . then he gives it a shake," Ethan said. "Once, twice . . ."

. . . third time's the charm, because . . .

". . . the next thing I hear is that bolt going *POP* as the lock comes undone, and he's opening the door with this big, shit-eating grin on his face."

All of that, and there's not a goddamn thing under that sink. Do you . . .

". . . remember that? Nothing but a bunch of old, dried-up mouse shit!" Ethan slapped his hand against the table and laughed loudly enough to draw glances from people at neighboring seats in the roadside diner. "Goddamn, those were good times."

One hour into their cross-country trek to Los Angeles spent recounting "good times" had been fun for Chris. Two hours listening to Ethan's stories had been mostly enjoyable, and three hours of it, moderately so. After five hours, however, Chris's patience had worn

7

thin. By now, ten hours deep, and another nineteen yet to go—not including the overnight detour they'd planned in Las Vegas—and he found himself ready to impale himself on his fork.

"You boys need anything else?" Short and stout, their waitress wore her cinnamon-colored hair teased high and a shade too bright to be natural. Her name tag read *Lois*.

"Just the check, please," Chris said.

Lois pulled out her ticket pad. "Everything taste okay?"

Ethan smiled disarmingly. "Just like Mom used to make."

"You poor thing." She ripped off the bill, plopped it down on the table, then walked away.

While Ethan took care of the tab, Chris headed for the men's room. As he reached for the door, the adjacent one to the ladies' room swung open unexpectedly. Startled, he danced backwards as a young woman plowed nearly headlong into him.

"I'm sorry . . . !" she exclaimed in a startled, breathless rush, just as an older woman walked out behind her.

"Oh, my goodness, Jessie," she scolded. "Watch where you're going! You nearly knocked him over." With an apologetic smile, she added to Chris, "I'm so sorry. Are you alright?"

"I . . . I'm fine, ma'am," he replied, looking at the girl, Jessie, as he spoke. She was pretty enough to warrant more than a passing glance, with long, dark hair drooping in lank waves to her shoulders. The spaghetti straps of her white tank top were loose enough to promise no bra beneath, and a pair of low-slung blue jeans hugged the shapely curves of her hips.

"Come along now." The older woman caught Jessie by the crook of her elbow like she might have a naughty kid. "Let the young man by."

"It's alright . . ." Chris began, but his voice faltered as Jessie brushed past him, catching him by the hand. It was only for a second, but that was all she needed to press something into his palm, a wadded napkin she'd been carrying.

"Hey, man," Ethan called from the direction of the cash register. "You got fifteen cents?"

Chris looked down at the napkin, puzzled, then watched the older woman lead Jessie out of the diner. She glanced back at Chris, her dark eyes round and nearly pleading.

"Hey," Ethan said again, and this time, he reached over and punched Chris in the shoulder to get his attention. "Ground control to Major Tom. I asked if you've got fifteen cents. I don't want to bust a dollar."

"Uh, yeah. Sure." Reaching into the front pocket of his jeans, Chris pulled out some loose change. "Here."

Through one of the nearby windows, he could see Jessie and the woman crossing the parking lot together for an older model Winnebago. He and Ethan had both noticed it upon their arrival at the diner, if not because it was something straight out of a 1980s time capsule, perfectly, hideously preserved, than because of a bumper sticker on the vehicle's tail end: *HONK if you've been SAVED!*

Ethan had found this hilarious. "We should get one of those, a button or something you could wear at the hospital," he said, then busted out laughing. "Every time one of your patients rolls out of surgery, you could pinch them on the nose. You know . . ." And he demonstrated this to Chris. "Honk! You've been saved!"

While Ethan finished paying the bill, Chris looked down at the napkin Jessie had handed to him. It had been folded neatly and deliberately, the way notes were folded in grade school when students tried to surreptitiously pass them during class. Curious, he worked the edges loose and opened it.

HELP

The word, all caps and clumsy block letters, looked like it had been scrawled in blood. He cut his gaze again toward the diner window and watched the RV pull away, heading back for the interstate.

"What's that?" Ethan asked, pushing his wallet back into his pocket.

"I don't know," Chris replied, showing it to him.

"Where'd you get it?"

"That girl gave it to me a second ago."

Ethan frowned. "What girl?"

"The one in the tank top." With a pointed glance, Chris added, "No bra."

"Oh, yeah." Ethan handed the note back. "Well, that's weird."

"Yeah." Chris frowned as the Winnebago drove off. "You think she's in trouble?"

"Could be." Ethan blew a sour belch against the side of his fist and grimaced. "Especially if she had the lunch special."

"Maybe we should call the police," Chris said a half an hour later, when they were back on the road. He'd brought the note with him

9

from the diner, and time and again, found himself glancing down at it, drawn to the grim plea and those stark, crooked letters.

HELP

"What the hell for?" Ethan asked.

"What if she's been kidnapped?" Chris asked, and when Ethan rolled his eyes, he frowned. "What? You hear about human trafficking all the time on the news."

"Yeah? You hear about people getting punked, too." Ethan grabbed the note and crumpled it up. When he opened the window, moving to toss it out, Chris grabbed his arm.

"Hey, don't."

But Ethan opened his hand anyway. The wind, whipping past the side of the car at more than seventy miles-an-hour, snatched the note and whipped it away.

"What the hell, man?" Chris exclaimed. "Why'd you do that?"

"Because it's bullshit," Ethan replied, rolling his window back up. "That girl was just messing around. Would you forget about it already?"

But that was easier said than done, at least for Chris. As the day wore on, he tried to feign the appropriate interest as Ethan talked about their Vegas side-trip but still couldn't quite shake his nagging, lingering unease.

". . . so, I'm thinking we should go to the Sahara first," Ethan said. "Hit the craps tables, you know, maybe play a little blackjack, then check out the nudie bars. I've heard there's a bunch of them all lined up in a row. Trust me, man. A nice pair of double-Ds waving in your face is exactly what the doctor . . ." His voice faded and he frowned, leaning forward to look out the windshield. "Isn't that the same RV we saw back at the diner?"

"Where?"

"Right there." Ethan pointed ahead of them, toward the unmistakable brown-and-white Winnebago. "That is the same one. *HONK if you've been SAVED!*" His frown deepened. "Are you following them?"

"What? Don't be a dumbass." Chris feigned obliviousness. After all, the RV had held a good fifteen-, if not a twenty-minute lead ahead of them on the highway. But head start or not, it had apparently hit a cruising speed of less than the posted limit, so he figured it wasn't completely his fault they'd caught up to it.

"A dumbass, huh?" Ethan said as the Winnebago's right turn

signal came on when it neared an exit and Chris did the same.

"What? We need to fill up."

At the gas station, the RV pulled around the far side of the building toward bays designed for tractor trailers and other large vehicles. Chris rolled to a stop next to the regular pumps.

"Have you been following them this whole time?" Ethan demanded, annoyed now, folding his arms across his chest.

"Of course not."

"Good. Because I told you, that girl was just fucking with you." Ethan unfastened his seatbelt and reached for the car door. "I'm going to go take a piss. You want anything? A Coke? Some Cheetos to go with your paranoia?"

"Yeah," Chris replied, flipping him the bird. "Ha ha."

The afternoon sun was bright, the air dry and warm. He stood in the shade beneath the fueling island's overhang, trying to keep an eye on the Winnebago while letting the pump in his hand run. He watched as an older man got out on the driver's side to refill the camper while the woman crossed the parking lot for the convenience store. There was no sign of Jessie.

Out of the corner of his eye, he saw Ethan leave the store. To his bewildered surprise, rather than head back for their rental car, he instead strode boldly toward the Winnebago.

What is he doing?

The older man had been walking back to the driver's side door, but paused, turning when Ethan called out to him.

Shit, Chris thought, an inward groan. *Ethan, what the fuck are you doing?*

While he watched, Ethan chatted with the man, smiling broadly and offering sweeping gestures with his hands now and again to indicate the camper. When the woman emerged from the store, she, too, apparently exchanged introductions with Ethan. Then, with a flip of his hand in an affable wave, he strolled languidly back across the parking lot.

"Honk," he told Chris as he approached. "You've been saved, man."

"What the hell?" Chris exclaimed. "What were you doing?"

"I told you. Saving your ass," Ethan replied, opening a bottle of iced tea he'd bought and taking a long swig. "I wanted to prove to you that note was bullshit, so I went and talked to those folks. Their names are Bill and Libby Warner. Turns out, they're on their way back from a Bible convention in Utah. I told them my dad used to have an RV, and we'd travel all over the country every summer when I was a kid. Great Lakes, the Grand Canyon, Yellowstone, Disneyland—you name it."

Chris frowned. "Your dad didn't have an RV. He drove that piece of shit Buick."

"I know that," Ethan replied. "But *they* didn't. Anyway, they told me they like to travel around, too. Only they didn't have any kids to go with them. They never had any, you see." He took another swig of tea and glanced pointedly at Chris. "No kids," he said again.

"What about Jessie?"

Ethan shook his head. "I don't know. But the way they were talking, there's nobody else but the two of them."

They sat in the car for a long, quiet moment, with Chris relaxing, then tightening his grasp repeatedly on the steering wheel. Finally, with an aggravated sigh, he reached for the ignition. Ethan caught him by the wrist.

"This isn't about your dad, Chris," he said quietly.

Chris tried to laugh. "What? Where the hell did that come from? This doesn't have anything to do with my father."

"I know. I just said that."

"Then we're in agreement," Chris said, jerking his hand free so he could start the car. "So shut the fuck up, alright?"

He tried to maintain a careful distance between the car and the camper once they were underway again, if only to keep from rousing Ethan's suspicions once more. When the RV next turned off the highway, it was nearly dusk, and Chris again followed. The Winnebago stopped at a campground while he pulled into the parking lot of a motel across the street.

"What's up? I thought you wanted to drive straight through." Ethan had been catnapping in the passenger seat and winced as he sat up, blinking dazedly at the buzzing neon *VACANCY* sign flashing overhead.

"I changed my mind." Chris killed the engine and unbuckled his seatbelt. "I'm beat."

"Oh." Ethan shrugged once, then dubiously surveyed the front of the motel. "You couldn't find a Holiday Inn or something? This place looks like a shit hole."

Chris laughed. "No, it doesn't."

"Come on, man. Seriously? I can practically feel the bedbugs from here."

"Would you stop? My back's killing me. I need to get out of this car. Besides, we've got beer that's been in the cooler all day, remember?" Chris leaned over and pinched Ethan's nose. "Honk, man. We've been saved."

Ethan laughed, slapping his hand away. "Right on."

Once they'd checked in, Ethan stretched out on the bed, an opened beer bottle in hand and pay-per-view porno muted on the television while he called the latest in his endless string of girlfriends-du-jour.

"Is that the one from Christmas?" Chris asked when he'd hung up. "What was her name? Ellen?"

"You mean Erin? God, no. She didn't make it past Easter. This one's Melissa."

Polishing off a beer of his own, Chris tossed the bottle into the waste can, then rooted through the mostly melted ice chips to fish out another one.

"If you came around more often, you might know these things," Ethan remarked as Chris handed him a dripping bottle.

"I've been kind of busy."

"Yeah, I've noticed," Ethan said, twisting the cap off his beer. With a smile, he leaned forward, tapping his bottle neck into Chris's. "So how about you? Still seeing that one girl, the redhead?"

"Meredith? No." Tipping his head back, Chris took a swallow of beer. "She didn't last past Easter, either."

"What happened?"

Chris shrugged. "I've been kind of busy," he said again.

"Too busy for your friends," Ethan mused. "Too busy to keep a girl. Man, don't you ever get lonely?"

"I'm too busy." With a laugh, Chris took another long drink of beer. Because Ethan didn't laugh along with him, studying him instead as if he had those X-ray-vision sunglasses advertised in the back of old Spider-Man comics, he sighed. "Okay, fine. Yeah. Sometimes. Maybe. I don't know. Seriously, man. I don't have time to notice anymore."

"You think when you move out to California, you might find some?" Ethan asked. "Time, I mean."

"Not likely." Chris chuckled as he reclined against the headboard, his legs stretched out. "But I haven't got the cardiology fellowship yet. My interview's on Friday at UCLA."

"You'll get it, man. They'd be fucking nuts not to give it to you."

Chris glanced at him, oddly touched. "Thanks."

"Hey." Ethan shrugged, taking a swig of beer. "I know you've been busting your ass these past few years with medical school and everything. You're really doing alright. I always knew you would." Balancing the cap from his bottle against the pad of his thumb and using his index finger, he flicked it away, sending it flying toward the far corner of the room. "Just like I always knew I wouldn't."

"Bullshit," Chris said, but Ethan only shrugged again. "You're doing just fine."

Ethan mimed jerking himself off. "I'm the manager of a goddamn appliance store."

"Hey, I couldn't sell that shit."

"Yeah, because you're busy doing what, brain surgery?"

"Hearts," Chris corrected.

"Whatever. At least it matters. You don't show up for work and someone could drop dead. *HONK, you've been SAVED,* remember? Me, I skip out, and some Susie Dipshit Homemaker's gotta ask another clerk to help her pick out a goddamn matching washer-dryer set."

"Ethan . . ." Chris said, reaching out, touching his shoulder gently.

"What you do makes a difference." Ethan shrugged him away, his expression growing somewhat sorrowful as he polished off his beer. *"You* make a difference." With a glance, he added, "I'm proud of you, man."

Chris smiled. "Thanks."

Ethan cut him a glance. "And I've missed you, goddamn it."

Chris clapped him on the shoulder again, fondly. "Yeah, man. Me, too."

He dreamed that he was home again. Not the sparsely furnished apartment he seldom used for more than showering or changing his clothes, but the house he'd grown up in, his childhood home in the Bridgeport district of Chicago.

He heard a loud, sudden *THUMP,* something heavy hitting the floor. "Dad?" he called, because his mother had already left for work. He was twelve years old, an eighth grader at Saint Mary of the Angels, and it was his father's job to drive him to school every morning.

"Dad?"

He should have known, should have realized, should have *remembered*, but in the surreal world of the dream, he didn't. Instead, he went downstairs, curious but not necessarily alarmed. That is, until he saw his father lying face-down in the foyer.

"Dad!" Chris rushed down the stairs, taking them two and three at a time. It still hadn't occurred to him that he was a grown man now, not an adolescent boy. He didn't think about that, didn't think about anything and instead simply acted.

"Dad!" Grasping him by the shoulders, Chris turned him onto his back, then slid his fingertips beneath the fleshy shelf of his chin, searching for a pulse.

"Dad, hold on." Ripping open the front of his father's shirt, he exposed the white, soft bulge of his belly. Lacing his fingers together, he pushed the heel of one hand atop the graying strands of wiry hair nestled over his dad's sternum. "Hold on," he said again, straightening his arms, leaning forward to begin chest compressions. "I can fix this, Dad. I can fix it, just hold on."

He woke with a start and a throbbing headache. The digital bedside clock read 5:37.

In the neighboring bed, Ethan remained fast asleep and snoring. The two had stayed up until well past midnight, drinking more than six beers apiece, along with the better part of a pint of whiskey Ethan had dug out of his suitcase. To the best of Chris's recollection, his friend's endless litany of stories about their youth had seemed not only bearable, but damn near entertaining the more drunk he'd become.

Which is probably why I was dreaming about Chicago, he thought. *And Dad.*

Limping to his feet, he shuffled into the bathroom. Planting one hand against the wall behind the toilet and holding his dick in the other, he pissed for what felt like an hour. After that, he found a four-cup coffee maker on the countertop by the vanity sink, but only decaffeinated packets to be made.

"Shit," he muttered, because if ever there had been a morning in which he needed a loaded cup of joe, it was that one. With a yawn and a scowl, he left Ethan sleeping in the room, and headed for the motel office in search of caffeine.

"Sorry, mister," the kid behind the front desk told him. "Just gave the last packet out about ten minutes ago."

Great. Chris resisted the urge to beat his forehead against the counter.

"You might try across the street at the RV campground," the kid suggested. "The guy who owns this place, that's his, too. They've probably got extra packs in the office. Just tell them you're staying here."

Chris jogged across the highway, waiting long enough for a tractor trailer to barrel past, loaded with livestock, judging by the pungent stink of manure left in its wake. Wind from its passage buffeted him, rocking him back and forth.

It was early enough for most anyone with common sense to still be blissfully asleep, and thus, there was little activity in the campground. To his surprise, as he walked toward the office, he saw Bill and Libby Warner approaching from the opposite direction, both carrying towels and toiletries on their way to the bathhouse.

Shit, he thought, turning quickly and pretending to read the announcements on a nearby bulletin board. He doubted either of them would recognize him, especially in the dark, but decided not to take any chances. Out of the corner of his gaze, he watched the couple part at the bathhouse entrance, Bill for the men's side and Libby for the other, and once they had disappeared inside, Chris took off. His mission to find coffee forgotten, he instead retraced their steps in search of the old Winnebago. It didn't take him long to find it, much less to decide.

I'm going in there.

He knew Ethan would shit a brick if he found out, and if he'd been there with Chris, he'd have said he was nuts. Nonetheless, Chris was determined to try. All he could think of was Jessie and how she'd looked at him in the diner with a sort of inexplicable but apparent distress.

She looked scared, like she was in trouble. I have to help her.

He paced a slow, cautious circle around the RV, pausing now and again to vainly peek in the windows. All of the curtains had been tightly drawn, and he glimpsed no hint of movement from inside, heard no noises—no TV, radio, nothing.

Sucking in a deep breath to steel himself, he reached up and caught the door handle. It was locked.

Now what? None of the windows had been open to his observation, not even a crack. The entire camper was sealed up tightly and the Warners would probably be back any second.

Not to mention Ethan's going to be waking up soon, wondering where in the hell I am.

Thinking of Ethan gave Chris an idea and he dipped his hand into his back pocket, pulling out his wallet.

Remember the time Mikey busted us into his uncle's house to get that fifth of Jack he swore was hidden underneath the kitchen sink? Using nothing but his goddamn driver's permit, you remember that?

Chris drew out his driver's license and stuck it between his teeth while he jammed the wallet back into his pocket. He'd never actually tried Mikey's lockpicking methods for himself, primarily because any time they'd needed them in his youth, Mikey had been around to employ them. It had never seemed too hard or taken too long, though, to the best of his recollection.

He jimmies it between the door and the jamb, Ethan had told him, and Chris shot a wary look around him then, shoulders hunched to disguise what he was doing, slipped the edge of his license into the slim margin of space between the door and its frame.

Gives it a wiggle or two to wedge it underneath the bolt, Ethan had said, but Chris found it took at least five or six before he was able to get it into place.

Then he gives it a shake, Ethan had said, and Chris did this, counting softly to himself.

"Once, twice, three time's the charm," he whispered, and his eyes widened in surprise as he heard a distinctive *CLACK,* the door unlocking.

"I'll be goddamned," he whispered with a shaky laugh. *I owe you one, Mikey.*

He stepped inside the camper and found himself facing a small kitchenette. Fishing his phone from his pocket, he thumbed on the light, panning the dim beam slowly to gather his bearings. To his right, he saw a living room area and, beyond it, the dashboard and driver's seat. An air freshener shaped like a cross dangled from the rearview mirror. On the left, a plastic, accordion-style door had been pulled shut, obscuring the rear sleeping compartment.

"Hello?" he called softly, hesitantly. "Jessie, are you in here?"

Nothing but silence in reply. The air felt thick and heavy inside the camper and had a strange odor about it, like maybe a mouse or something had died in one of the cupboards and started to rot.

"Jessie?" he tried again, but still no response.

Get out, he told himself. *Ethan was right. She's not here. You need to get out—right now.*

But then he thought of that little note, carefully folded and written in blood, begging for help, and the fear he'd seen in Jessie's eyes, and knew he couldn't. Not yet.

Not until I'm sure.

He pulled the accordion door back and looked inside the sleeping compartment. Here, a twin-sized mattress sat flush against the back wall of the camper, the rear window above it, curtains closed. He saw something in the bed, a small, shadow-draped figure.

"Jessie?" Seized with adrenaline, he hurried across the room, not knowing what he meant to do, maybe scoop her up in his arms and carry her out of there, back to the motel with him, like some kind of lame-ass hero in a cheesy movie. "Jessie," he began, reaching down. "Jessie, can you—"

His voice cut short when he touched her. Judging by how cold and stiff she felt, she'd been dead for at least the better part of the day, long enough for rigor mortis to have fully set in. As the light from his phone fell across her, he saw she'd been flayed, every discernable inch of her skin stripped away with gruesome, surgical precision, leaving only raw, glistening meat behind. Her eyes bulged from the confines of their lidless sockets, and because her lips had been cut away, her jaw hung lax and ajar, as if frozen in a shriek.

Clapping his hand over his mouth, Chris felt his stomach give a queasy lurch. "Oh, Jesus . . . !" he gulped, staggering backwards, floundering into what felt like a heavy curtain. Not until he turned around, the phone light bobbing unsteadily in his hand, did he realize what it was.

Like a hand-washed garment hung on a line to dry, Jessie's skin dangled from a series of hooks affixed into the camper ceiling. Everything somehow seemed to be intact, as if it had been cut open along invisible seams, then peeled meticulously away from muscle and bone. Her limbs dangled in lank, fleshy folds, her face toward the sagging remnants of her belly and breasts, her hair still affixed to her scalp.

Oh Jesus! Chris wheeled around and puked up the last of the previous night's beer. His phone tumbled from his hand, the light winking out, plunging him into darkness.

Oh, Jesus, he thought again in a terrified panic, reaching blindly for it, fumbling around on the floor. *Oh, Jesus, oh fuck oh HOLY*

FUCKING CHRIST these people are crazy! I have to get out of here! I have to—

He heard the floor creak and the snap of a switch, and suddenly, the back room of the Winnebago flooded with fluorescent light. With a startled cry, Chris whirled, then backpedaled in stricken alarm.

"Well, look who it is, Bill," Libby Warner said, standing in the doorway beside her husband, smiling as if pleasantly surprised. "One of those nice boys from yesterday. I told you they were following us."

"How the hell did he get in?" Bill asked, turning to shoot her an accusatory glare. "Did you forget to lock the door again?"

"Well, of course not," she replied. "You stood there and watched me—"

She uttered a yelp as Chris charged the doorway, knocking her aside and plowing Bill off his feet. As the old man crashed down onto his ass, Chris stumbled past, making a frantic break for the front door. Just as he reached for it, meaning to shove it open wide and run like hell, something slammed into him from behind, catching him between the shoulder blades. It felt like an arrow fired from a crossbow, striking hard and sinking deep, punching through vertebrae and severing his spinal cord in an instant. He felt his legs abruptly give out from under him and, like a marionette with its strings cut, he collapsed.

"Goddamn it, Libby," Bill exclaimed. "Why'd you do that?"

"I couldn't very well let him go, now could I?" she replied. "Besides, I have a new one, and now you do, too. We'll be a matching set."

Chris groaned, unable to move. Everything from that brutal point of impact in his back on downward felt leaden and numb. He managed to turn his head enough to look behind him, and by the light in the bedroom, he could see what had struck him: a long, spindly, articulated appendage that had burst from the base of Libby's right hand. She held her arm out toward Chris, with the skin of her wrist split in a wide gash. The bizarre, bloody proboscis waggled in the open air between them like a grotesque extra limb.

"But I don't want this one," Bill said, sounding irritable. "I liked his friend better, the one who came up to us at the gas station."

"Beggars can't be choosers," Libby chided. "He'll do just fine. Look how young he is." With a grunt, she yanked the protrusion loose from Chris's back, and it dangled, twitching, from her arm. "And so handsome, too."

"His friend was roomier," Bill complained. "You know I hate it when they ride up on me."

"Beggars can't be choosers," Libby told him again. "Why don't you at least try him on and see how he fits? If you still don't like him after that, I'll catch the other one for you."

Bill heaved a put-upon sigh. "Fine."

Bill's entire face began to sag as, with a moist, squelching sound, he dragged it off like an ill-fitting rubber Halloween mask. What lay beneath wasn't remotely human. It was monstrous, with black, glittering eyes and a gaping mouthful of jagged, pointed teeth.

Chris tried to scream but couldn't. "What . . . are you?" he moaned as Libby lifted her arm and, with it, the whip-like length of bony protuberance. Now he could see the distal-most end of it and the part that had struck him—a long, wicked spike, like the stinger on a scorpion's tail. As she leveled this at his head, drawing it back to strike, he clamped his eyes shut. "Oh . . . oh, Jesus . . . *what the fuck are you?*"

By the time Ethan woke, it was nearly ten o'clock. He found himself alone in the motel room, much to his bewildered surprise, and after poking his head vainly into the bathroom, calling Chris's name, he wandered down to the office to search for him.

"I think he went across the street," the clerk said, pointing out the window. "He said he wanted to get some coffee."

"Huh." Ethan scratched his head, puzzled. "I guess I'll wait for him, then."

"Checkout's at eleven," the kid reminded as he walked toward the door.

"Guess I won't be waiting long," Ethan muttered. Pulling out his cell phone, he sent a quick text to Chris: *Hey, dumbass, where are you? It's time to roll.*

He stopped at a soda machine to buy a can of Mountain Dew. As he cracked it open, he looked out toward the nearby ribbon of highway and watched a couple of tractor trailers go by. Beyond them, across the road, he saw an RV campground and, pulling out of the entrance, a familiar sight—that piece of shit Winnebago Chris had been going on about all yesterday afternoon. Although Ethan stood too far away to make out who might be behind the wheel, there was no mistaking either it or the ridiculous bumper sticker on the back: *HONK if you've been SAVED!*

As the camper drove past, he lifted his hand in greeting. He still didn't get why Chris had been so worked up. After all, the old folks driving it had seemed harmless enough.

Nice, even, he thought, as he looked at his phone and waited with mounting impatience for Chris to reply.

SUMMERS WITH ANNIE
Greg Sisco

"SURE BEATS DRIVING, DOESN'T IT?" said Dad as we stood on the edge of the ferry. I had my feet on the lower rail and my arms folded over the upper one, leaning out to watch the sea go by.

It was the summer before I started the first grade. The summer after Mom left.

I think I missed her in those days, then for a while I resented her, but before long it was what it was. Life has a funny way of doing that. Something that crashes your world down one year is a scar you don't think about the next, and something you pass without a second glance today, you realize tomorrow it meant the world.

I'm an old man now, and my mother's story and mine never again crossed paths. No one ever told me details and I can't remember precisely how she left or why, though I do know that when I got older and tried my first beer, it smelled like her, and considering she left in 1933 when Prohibition was still in swing, I suspect her departure and her smell may have been in some way related.

We didn't take many photographs back then, and I don't have one of Mom. To tell the truth, I have no idea what my mother looked like. That pleasant but troublesome smell is all I have left of her.

But this isn't Mom's story.

"That's it. Way, way out there," said Dad, pointing. "Way out on the horizon. You can just make out a few trees. Can you see it?"

"Oh yeah!" I lied.

"No you can't," said Dad. "There's nothing out there. The island's the other way, behind you."

I looked up from my perch on the rail and he looked down, grinning a playful smile, having caught me in a lie, his teeth yellowed by a lifetime of smoking. There was wind blowing his hair back, his skin was slightly sunburned, and the collar of his shirt had blown up on one side.

I don't know what triggers our young brains to take those early snapshots for our memories, or why I remember Dad laughing at me that day but I don't remember Mom walking out. I just know that my earliest visual memory is that image of Dad, looking down at me with that yellow smoker's smile in the summer wind.

Of Dad, I have a picture; of Mom, I have a smell.

But I'm glad my young memory chose to take a picture of Dad that day, because it's the only one I had time to get.

Dragging our suitcases across the boardwalk with the beach at our side and salty air in our noses, it was a matter of minutes before Dad spotted the Cecil House—a freshly-painted and colorful building, extravagant and out-of-place amidst the unfinished adobe that made up most of the island's architecture. It was the island's only movie house.

Ostentatious as it was, the Cecil House didn't need to stand out to pull in Dad and me. Ever since I was born, the movies have a way of making themselves known at all my key moments. For instance, on October 26th, 1927, *The Jazz Singer* became the first movie released with pre-recorded sound, ushering in the era of the talkie and changing cinema forever. That was the day Mom and Dad held baby me in their arms for the first time.

I'd bet good money Dad knew that fact. He probably even told it to me, though I would have been too young to appreciate it at the time. If he'd been around longer, I'm sure he would have told it to me again and again, because something Dad and I ended up with in common, one of the few things I remember about him, is that Dad was a tried-and-true, card-carrying, dyed-in-the-wool movie-lover.

I was five going on six that summer. I was seeing a beach for my first time, excited out of my wits to swim in the ocean, build a sandcastle, and ride a merry-go-round, and there was Dad, pointing to a movie house and saying, "Ooh, should we see what's playing?"

He always asked that question when we passed a movie house. It didn't matter if we'd already passed it and checked an hour ago. He had to make sure nothing had changed. Most of the time, even if we'd already seen whatever was playing, we ended up inside. Even despite the sunny beaches and the summer air, this day was no different.

One man and one girl ran the Cecil House back then. The man must have been ninety years old, walking with a cane but still spry and chipper. The girl was about my age. It seemed the old man ran everything himself, except that once the movie started, he stayed in the projection booth and the girl held down the lobby.

"*Summers with Annie*," said the old man when my father asked what tonight's show was. "There's a matinee in fifteen minutes and tonight's show is at seven-thirty."

"I've never heard of *Summers with Annie*," said Dad. "What's it about?"

"Couple of kids who fall in love a little more each summer," said the old man. "It's cornball stuff, you ask me. But they shot it here on the island, so I guess that draws people in."

It sure drew Dad in. He said it was divine providence we happened by. Still hauling our bags from the ferry and only halfway to the hotel, he bought us each a ticket for the matinee. We checked our bags, which you could do in those days, and the old man helped the little girl count out change for a popcorn and a soft drink each.

As I said, movies have always popped their heads in on me for my key moments, but no movie ever got involved in my life in quite the way *Summers with Annie* did.

Here is *Summers with Annie*, the abridged version:

A thirteen-year-old boy named Colin goes to an island with his family against his will. He hates it until he meets a girl named Annie who lives there. They have fun for the summer, each feeling their first spark of romance, until summer ends, and Colin leaves.

So sad.

Colin comes back the next year excited to see Annie, but discovers she found a new beau in the seasons that passed. He hangs around with her as a friend, but feels like he missed his chance.

Again, so sad.

Colin comes back a third year and this time he brings his new girlfriend, Betsy, thinking they'll go on double dates. He finds out Annie broke up with her fella and she was hoping they'd get together this year.

A third time, so sad.

Colin marries Betsy and they move to the island. Betsy gets sick and dies. Colin meets Annie again and finally marries her.

So . . . happy?

I didn't know the phrase "glossed-over" when I was five, but I knew it when I saw it. As the characters threw their big, swinging, fire-dancing party of a wedding, celebrating and smiling, I remember a sick feeling in my stomach. I thought, *Betsy is dead. Isn't anyone sad?*

The wedding party scene went on forever. It seemed like an hour of dancing, singing, and celebrating until it was so boring I couldn't keep my eyes open. I fell asleep and missed the ending. What I took out of it was that Betsy died and Colin and Annie celebrated forever. I never knew a happy ending could feel so cruel.

Like most movies of the era, the credits in *Summers with Annie* ran at the beginning rather than the end. When the movie was over, "The End" appeared on screen and the house lights came up. The audience stood and I roused from my sleep to find Dad wasn't next to me. His empty popcorn bag and drink cup were sitting by his chair, but the chair was empty. I assumed he was in the men's room and settled into my seat.

After a few minutes had gone by, the old man and the little girl came into the theater to clean up. I felt weird sitting there while they cleaned, so I got up to see if I could find Dad. He wasn't in the men's room, or the lobby, or outside.

I went back to the auditorium, thinking maybe he'd slipped past me somehow and went to look for me in my seat.

"Was my Dad just in here looking for me?" I asked.

The old man looked up from where he was sweeping. "No. Where'd you last see him?"

"I fell asleep in the movie."

Something happened that lasted less than a second and that I struggle to describe. It was as simple as a pause registering on the old man's face. Maybe his eyes widened or his skin paled, maybe his breath changed, but in some barely significant way, I felt his fear.

Don't misunderstand me. I am as old now as he was then, and I have children and grandchildren and I know the fear that tightens within you when a child tells you, "I am lost." I can't tell you how I knew, especially not back then, but the fear on the old man's face was not that fear. It was deeper, more personal.

He came up the stairs quickly, not using his cane, and took me by the hand. "Let's see if we can find him, shall we?"

Of course, we couldn't.

His cold, stiff hand gripping mine, the old man pulled me up and down stairs, through doors, down halls, calling out my father's name, insisting I call out with him. The old man was more frantic even than I was.

As the sun went down, I sat on the boardwalk outside the Cecil House, crying softly and listening to the tide. The little girl, a sweetheart, sat beside me and held my hand until a policeman came and took me to the station. The policeman's manner, with that too-friendly voice an adult puts on when they try to calm a child, only chilled me more.

I never checked into the hotel that night, and I didn't get to spend my summer on the island. I never even found out what became of our suitcases.

A little over ten years later, however, I did learn what the old man was thinking in that frozen moment of fear.

Let's go back to the movies. Let me tell you the story of a boy who grew up with them.

During the Christmas season of 1933, this boy left the home of his foster parents and snuck into a movie house. He'd been feeling empty and lonely and struggling to cope. He missed his father, and every time he walked by a movie house, he'd say to his foster parents, "Ooh, should we see what's playing?" the way his father used to say to him, but the foster parents always said no. So finally, the boy snuck in by himself and watched *King Kong*, and for the first time since his dad disappeared, he felt happy.

This became the boy's tradition, waiting at the emergency exit to slide in when somebody left, and then hiding in the theater until the next show started. He did this until 1935, when an usher caught him waiting for *Bride of Frankenstein* and dragged him to the manager, who screamed at him and threatened to call his foster parents.

After that, the boy stole. Mostly he took candy from stores and sold it at school, using the money to buy tickets to the movies multiple times per week, seeing everything over and over and over. This continued until mid-1936 when the theater manager had a chance conversation with the boy's foster father and mentioned how often the boy was at the theater. The foster father demanded the boy tell him where the money came from. Then he beat the boy so badly that the boy was removed from his care, a remarkable feat in 1936 when child-beating was the prevailing American pastime. Fittingly, the last movie the boy stole his way into was Charlie Chaplin's *Modern Times*, the last major release to use silent film conventions, considered to be the final movie of the silent film era. The boy was born on the day of the first talking picture, and on the day of the last silent film, he grew up.

At the orphanage they didn't go to the movies, and for a few years depression set in for the boy. He got into fights, he stole and vandalized property, and was generally considered a troubled child until he left the orphanage in 1939 at the age of twelve. He left of his own volition and with little protest from the adults, who were as tired of him as he was of them.

He presented himself politely to Mr. Anniston, the manager of the movie theater, who agreed to feed him and let him sleep on a mattress in the projection booth in exchange for helping to sell tickets and concessions. Moreover, he would be allowed to watch all the movies he wanted for free.

The boy took to the work with pleasure. He watched the regulars come and go. More than the rest, he watched Ruthie van Aken who went to the movies every Friday with her boyfriend and ordered a Cherry Coke and a popcorn with a smile he found himself looking forward to, right from his first week working, when she came to see *The Wizard of Oz* (contrary to what some people tell you, not the first color film, but oh was it like seeing in color for the first time when the boy laid eyes on Ruthie).

There were no multiplexes back then, and new films weren't being released every week the way they are today. The people who came every week were that certain breed of people who love to watch a movie, even a bad movie, more than they love to do anything else. The boy was one of those people and so, it seemed, was Ruthie.

When Ruthie began coming in without her boyfriend and—after being prodded in an attemptedly offhanded tone—admitted that they had broken up, it was with the second-most fear the boy had ever felt in a theater that he asked her if he could sit next to her and if they could watch the movie together. Mr. Anniston, by now viewing the formerly troubled boy's transformation as the great deed of his life, was more than happy to cover at the concession stand while the boy watched *Citizen Kane* on his first date.

This is what I mean when I say the movies have always made themselves known for my big moments. I saw plenty of bad ones too, of course, plenty of movies that today are lost to history and have no reason to be rediscovered. But for some reason, me and the movies, we always had our big moments together.

Ruthie and I were only fifteen, young even for the time, the day I got down on one knee in the theater and asked her to marry me. She said yes, and we were overheard by enough nearby patrons who were in the process of exiting that a round of cheers broke out when we kissed.

You guessed it. *Casablanca*.

Ruthie and I grew up in a quiet coastal town where vacation was one of three things. If you were well-off, you took a plane to any number of exciting places the world had to offer for the people it favored. If you were dirt poor, you pitched a tent on the beach a few miles out of town where no one would pester you and you could cook on a fire and make love in the open air. If you were in the middle, you went to the island.

Ruthie and I were dirt poor, so when we went off to be together, we usually pitched a tent. But Mr. Anniston and I had come to develop one of those not-really-a-father, not-really-a-son, but-close-enough-strangers-might-miss-it relationships. He wasn't rich, but he wasn't poor either, and when I married Ruthie, he wanted us to have a proper honeymoon. That's how, ten years after Dad's disappearance, almost to the day, I found myself in the familiar position of standing on a ferry with my favorite person in the world.

"When was the last time you went?" I asked Ruthie.

"I only went once. I think I was eight or nine? How old were you again?"

"Five."

"Wow. That must have been really rough, what you went through."

"I don't remember it too well."

I put my elbows on the railing and looked down at the water, hoping the moment would pass without us having to talk about it. We'd had the conversation in depth once, a few months ago, or at least what little depth there was to be had. You can't talk about something like that without people pouring pity all over you and making you feel worse about it than you want to. Most of the time it's easier to keep it as your own.

"That's it up there," I said, pointing, before she could ask me anything more. "You see it? Those trees on the horizon?"

She squinted. "I don't think so."

"Yeah, it's not there," I said. "Thought I could getcha."

She looked back at me with a smile, wind blowing her hair back, skin slightly sunburned.

Come to think of it, as I tell this story now, I don't know if that image of Dad was always burned into my memory, or if it came back to me as déjà vu in that moment I looked at Ruthie.

One way or the other, I'll never forget either of them.

I remembered the Cecil House being on the main road facing the beach, so I said, "You've seen one beach, you've seen them all. Let's walk a street or two back and take in the island."

It wasn't that I hoped to avoid the Cecil House altogether. I just wasn't ready yet. The ferry ride, the island, the walk to the hotel. There was a heaviness to each step that brought me closer, and I thought, even if it was stupid, that I'd feel a little better looking at the place if we didn't have our bags with us the way Dad and I did. I didn't want us to be fresh off the boat and with the whole trip ahead of us. I wanted us settled and comfortable.

The truth is, I actually looked forward to revisiting the Cecil House on this trip, just not right away. Sitting with my bride in the same theater where I last sat with my father was a bittersweet idea I looked forward to cherishing as a memory, but it had to be done on my terms.

So we checked into the hotel. We drank at cabana bars that broke liquor laws for newlyweds. We rented a tandem bicycle, which on the mainland was a fad that had passed us by, but here on the island was a novelty catering to tourists like us who'd missed it when it was popular.

It didn't ride well. It was awkward and uncomfortable and we each put panicked feet on the ground every few minutes and eventually crashed it in the dirt before walking it back to the rental shop. At sundown we stumbled on sore and scraped legs, wobbly from the booze, barefoot in the sand. We held each other up and watched artists fire dance for the tourists and I thought I'd never be this happy again.

"Ooh! Look!" Ruthie shouted suddenly, grabbing my hand in

both of hers. "It's a movie we haven't seen!"

She was looking up at a marquee above the Cecil House. And even though I'd been looking forward to watching a movie there with my arm around Ruthie, I felt my stomach twist itself in a knot when I saw that, all these years later, they were still playing *Summers with Annie.*

"We have to go see it! Let's see if we're in time for tonight's show!"

How could I say no? How could I kill her bright and exciting moment by bringing my long-gone father into this up-until-recently-perfect night? And in the same way I thought it bittersweet the idea of sitting with my bride in the theater where I sat with Dad, wouldn't it be that much more bittersweet if we watched the same movie? I had no logical reason to protest, and yet something in my chest was objecting. Something said, *Don't go back in that movie house.*

But I was also sixteen and in love. And when fear squeezes the heart and a pretty girl squeezes the hand, for youth, the choice makes itself.

Some people say you haven't seen a movie until you've seen it twice. The second viewing often casts things in a new light that you didn't appreciate during the first. It's also true that perspectives shift as time goes on. The five-year-old boy and the sixteen-year-old man who watched *Summers with Annie* at the Cecil House were two different people and they saw it through two different sets of eyes. We've all read a book or seen a movie or heard a song, and then have come back to it ten years later with a new perspective. We've all thought, "I can't believe this is the same movie."

But when it came to *Summers with Annie*, it *wasn't* the same.

Most of it I could have attributed to faulty memory. I was barely old enough to even have memories the last time I watched it, although the traumatic night made it stick out a little more than it might have otherwise. I could have looked past how the actors were older than I remembered, or how the island setting, lost in time and difficult to pin down, seemed to echo fashions closer to now than to ten years ago when I first saw it, and I certainly could have easily written off the eerie coincidence of the tandem bike scene of which I had no recollection.

I could have let a million things go. Maybe I even could have let the overall production value go—the fact that, whatever it was, the film processing, or the cameras—whatever separated the look of a 1933 film from a 1944 one, this one looked distinctly more like the latter.

But I clearly remembered sitting in that theater at the age of five and thinking, *Betsy is dead. Isn't anyone sad?*

In this version, her name wasn't Betsy.

It was Ruthie.

I held my wife's hand as tight as I could without hurting her, that fear in my chest building with each frame of the movie until her death scene, only finally settling down a little when the death was over and Ruthie was still holding my hand.

As the movie neared its end, my memories of that day from ten years ago pushed harder to the forefront of my mind. The wedding scene once again made me drowsy. Whether it was the booze, the bellyful of popcorn, or the drawn-out film editing, as the islanders threw their party and danced in the streets, I struggled to keep my eyes open.

Not happening, I thought. *I refuse to fall asleep in this movie again. I don't care if this reception scene lasts another hour. I will sit here and watch the ending I never saw as a child and then Ruthie and I will get up and leave and go back to the hotel.*

Then the movie changed again.

Even though I never saw this part as a child, I knew it changed. It had to have changed. Because what was on screen was impossible. It was impossible even today, but it was twice as impossible ten years ago.

Among the island celebration, tending bar on the beach, handing drinks to two bikini-clad tourists, was Dad.

I woke up in the theater. One of those falling sensations that brings you back from a nightmare. I jerked forward and almost fell out of the seat onto the floor with the spilled popcorn and the shoe prints.

But no. This wasn't how nightmares work. When you wake from a nightmare, things are supposed to be better, not worse.

Ruthie was gone. The movie was over. The theater was empty.

I stood up fast, all the blood running down to my feet and my hands shaking. My heart was beating so loudly my ears hurt.

Take it easy. She's just in the bathroom. You were drunk, you fell asleep during the movie, and you had a nightmare. Of course you did, given your history with the movie. What else would happen? You fell asleep thinking about Dad.

Except I didn't fall asleep.

I was drowsy. My eyes were heavy, but I never got that close to sleep, not really. It was too important. There was too much fear in me.

Of course there was fear. That's why you had the nightmare.

I ran.

I ran full sprint out of the auditorium, past the ushers who were coming. I burst straight through the door to the ladies' room without knocking, pushing open stall doors. I wasn't thinking. Even with that voice in my head trying to calm me down, trying to reason with me, I was out of control.

But I didn't walk in on anybody. Certainly not Ruthie.

"No," I muttered into my hands, collapsing against the wall outside the ladies' room door. "No, no, no! No!"

I looked up from where I was sitting and a woman about sixteen years old was looking down at me, a fear on her face that was probably just rubbing off from my own fear. She looked familiar. It took me a moment to remember the old man and the little girl who had let us in last time I was here. That old man who'd seemed to know, even before I did, that Dad was gone and he wasn't coming back. And the little girl who held my hand while I waited for a new life.

I leapt to my feet and grabbed her by the shoulders.

"The old man! Is the old man here?"

"What?"

"When I was a kid and I was here, you were with an old man. Your grandpa or something. He knew what this was. I need to talk to him. Where is he?"

"He died. He died years ago."

I hung my head, the tears starting to form. "I need to know what happened to my wife," I whispered.

She hugged me and I sobbed into her shoulder. A few minutes later, she walked me out of the building and sat with me on the boardwalk, looking out at the ocean with me, and holding my hand in that all too familiar way.

She asked me my name.

"Colin," I said. "Like the boy in the movie."

She hesitated, then said, "I'm Annie."

Annie's mother died when she was a baby, probably in childbirth, though Annie was spared the details. Much like me, when she was barely old enough to form memories, her father disappeared. She was left under the care of an old man she called Pawpaw, who was her grandfather or maybe even her great-grandfather, though Annie never thought to ask and Pawpaw never thought to say.

Pawpaw had lived on the island since he was born, helping to run a theater with his father and his own pawpaw.

Back then the theater was called the Bannister House, which Pawpaw's pawpaw claimed was because the famous playwright Nathaniel Bannister had visited the island on the summer vacations of his childhood years and had staged some of his earliest work here. Pawpaw had always been skeptical of his pawpaw's claims, and when they repurposed the theater for film instead of plays, it was a happy coincidence that a child who used to act in community theater had grown up to be Cecil B. DeMille, so Pawpaw changed the name to the Cecil House.

That was the legend, though Annie doubted there was any more truth to the DeMille story than to the Bannister one. Annie was skeptical about a lot of Pawpaw's stories. And though she would have liked to write Pawpaw off as an eccentric kook, and for the most part was able to do so, there was one story Pawpaw told that did not fit the mold of the other tall tales with which he so loved to regale her. This other story was not a story dreamed up by a man wanting attention. It was a story by a man haunted with anguish and despair.

As Pawpaw told it, in 1916, when film was still new to the Bannister House, a film had been brought to the theater which had supposedly been shot on the island, though no one on the island remembered it having happened. The movie was called *Summers with Annie*, and it was about a boy and a girl falling in love over the summers of their childhood.

It was a silent film.

Pawpaw watched it with his wife, Mawmaw, who disappeared during the screening. He mourned her loss, eventually letting go, and each summer when the theater played the movie again, he declined to revisit the painful memory of the first time he watched it, calling it cornball stuff for the tourists.

Enter Annie's father, Bruce.

In 1930, when sound on film was a new concept, a print of *Summers with Annie* arrived for the summer season with sound. Bruce ventured that it was simply a new film of the same title, or the same film remade for sound. But it bothered Pawpaw. And it bothered him even more when the film began playing for audiences, and through glimpses of the film, Pawpaw could confirm that it was indeed the same movie, shot right there on the island.

Film with sound was a new concept in 1930. A film shot with sound here on the island would have drawn attention; it would have been a novelty. It hadn't happened. Furthermore, he remembered specific shots, specific compositions, specific actors, and he was positive this was not a film remade for sound. This was the same film, only different.

Bruce said, "Let's watch it. If you're going to let it occupy this much of your mind, I'll run the projector and you sit in the theater, or you run the projector and I'll sit in the theater, and we'll watch the movie and put it behind us."

Pawpaw agreed. Bruce ran the projector and Pawpaw sat in the theater, and he watched four reels of *Summers with Annie*, trying to understand how this silent film had become a talkie.

When the fourth reel ended, Bruce failed to make the changeover from the projection booth.

Pawpaw never found Bruce.

He found Mawmaw though. She was in the movie, dancing at a party with other islanders.

Pawpaw closed the theater for what he believed was the first time ever. But everywhere he went, he felt he was in the movie. Wedding parties, events, people who looked like the actors or the extras. They were always in his periphery, there for an instant and gone when he looked again. He was driven mad.

Giving in to what he saw as the movie's threats against him, he reopened the theater and his feelings of paranoia went away. He continued to show *Summers with Annie* to audiences, but refused to watch for more than the few seconds required of him to make the reel changes. He forbade Annie to enter the auditorium or the projection booth when the movie was playing, so she stayed in the lobby while he ran the projector.

One night in 1933 a little boy came into the auditorium while Pawpaw and Annie were cleaning, crying that his father had disappeared. Pawpaw took the boy to look, and even that five-year-old boy could see that Pawpaw was the more frightened of the two of them.

Drunk and crying, a few hours after the police took the boy away, that was the night Pawpaw finally told all this to Annie, sitting on the boardwalk outside the Cecil House, in the same place Annie would tell it to me years later.

Annie went home and slept. The next morning she couldn't find Pawpaw, but in the projection booth of the Cecil House, four reels of *Summers with Annie* had been played and the fifth was still queued.

Annie and I had an island wedding with fire dancers and a cabana bar. I kept looking around, hoping to spot Dad bartending, or Ruthie smiling in approval, or Pawpaw giving me a look that said I better take good care of her, but I didn't see any of that. It was just a wedding.

We sold the Cecil House and left the island. We haven't been back since.

Today it's probably the Spielberg House.

For over seventy years since, Annie and I have made each other happy. While friends around us have married and divorced, fallen in and out of love, ridden roller coasters of moods, we've remained calmly and comfortably in love. Neither of us has ever once raised our voice, there have been no arguments to speak of, and friends have called our relationship supernatural.

I am inclined to agree.

Annie and I have three children. Their birthdays are *Miracle on 34th Street, Singin' in the Rain,* and *Rebel Without a Cause.* Annie's, by the way, is the same as mine.

Sometimes I catch myself feeling like I was given the incredible blessing of a perfect marriage, and I have to stop myself. I have to wonder how happy I might or might not have been with Ruthie. I have to remember the little boy who, at five years old, sat in a theater thinking, *Betsy is dead. Isn't anyone sad?*

I have to remember the ruthless happy ending even a five-year-old could find cruel, and I have to shiver.

But mostly I don't think about it.

Life has a way of doing that. Something that crashes your world down one year is a scar you don't think about the next, and something you pass without a second glance today, you realize tomorrow it meant the world.

Annie and I go to the movies every week. Once in a while, in a crowd scene, I'll see Dad back there having dinner, or tending bar, or sitting in traffic. Once in a while I'll see Ruthie too, answering a phone, or pushing a stroller, or crossing the street.

I hope they're happy wherever they are. They look it.

If you ask Annie whether she ever sees Pawpaw in the movies, she'll tell you no.

She'll tell you her husband is imaginative, quirky, and crazy as a loon but that's why she loves him. She'll tell you she's far less superstitious. She'll tell you the movies don't control our lives, and a movie certainly didn't take people away just so she and I could fall in love. She'll tell you she'd rather not talk about these things, or think about what happened to Pawpaw, or to our fathers, or to Ruthie, because the world is a scary place and it's probably not happy things that took those people away from us. But no. It wasn't the movies.

That's what she'll tell you.

But if you ask her whether she ever got around to watching *Summers with Annie*, she'll shake her head no.

EXPERTISE

Asher Ellis

THEY WERE ABOUT FIVE HUNDRED feet from the cay when Alberto heard his client's nervous voice erupt in the earpiece of his diving helmet.

"Alberto! I think a shark is following me!"

The scuba guide kicked his left foot to face the woman swimming behind him. At first, Alberto could only see the slender form of his client, Ms. Cynthia Reynard, churning her flippered feet as she turned her head backwards.

"I don't see any—"

The guide's voice immediately cut short when a long, sleek figure emerged from the murky darkness of the water. The creature appeared to be easily seven feet in length, a jagged fin resting upon its back. As it rose closer to the surface, the sunlight reflected off a smiling mouth of uneven, needle-like teeth.

"That's not a shark, Ms. Reynard," Alberto said calmly, identifying the pursuing fish. "It's just a harmless barracuda."

Cynthia, who had not taken her eye off the creeping predator, was now completely turned around and pedaling backwards.

"Harmless?" she yelled, unconvinced. "Look how big it is. And those teeth!"

Alberto swam back to close the distance between himself and his shaken client. "What you're looking at is what they call a Great

Barracuda, the largest of the species. It's not uncommon for them to grow over six feet in length. They *are* predators, but they only use those sharp teeth on smaller prey, like guppies and flounders."

Alberto reached Cynthia's side and stared at the carnivorous fish that followed them. He didn't bother telling Ms. Reynard that it was the biggest barracuda he'd ever seen, in either the ocean or in an aquarium. And that was saying something, considering out of all his knowledge of aquatic life, the barracuda was his area of expertise.

Instead, he added, "Wow! It looks like he's been eating well."

The barracuda shimmied its tail, and in the blink of an eye, darted five feet closer.

Cynthia shrieked and grabbed Alberto's arm. "Ah! It's coming for us!"

Alberto chuckled, "It's just curious. Barracudas are scavengers and often mistake humans as larger predators. He's just waiting for you to take down your prey so he can nibble at the leftovers."

And while what Alberto said was entirely true, he began to have doubts even as the words fell from his lips. The closer the barracuda approached, the more ambiguous its appearance became. Alberto had encountered several barracuda in his diving career, and none had been as unique as the specimen that trailed them now. Even with the bright rays of the high noon sun beaming down into the tropical water, the barracuda showed a surprising variation in color. Instead of the bluish, silver scales prevalent in the fish's species, this barracuda was stained a deep crimson hue.

A red barracuda? Perhaps Alberto had been mistaken all along, and this really was a young shark of some kind. But after the fish made another quick dart and closed its distance by five more feet, its distinct body shape eliminated any doubt in Alberto's mind.

"Why on earth would it mistake me for a predator?" Cynthia asked, trying to make light of a situation that obviously still frightened her. "It must know my ex-husband."

The attractive woman laughed at her own joke and Alberto joined in, all the while keeping a close eye on the lurking fish. Cynthia had previously told him all about her wealthy ex-spouse, a Wall Street investor who'd lost half his assets to her after a lengthy divorce. She was just the sort of clientele Alberto preferred: rich divorcees vacationing by themselves in hopes of getting over their old spouses by finding a handsome local to show them a good time. And with Alberto's suave Italian heritage, catching these gold-digging beauties was easier than fishing for anything found in the ocean. A private scuba diving tour, which meant two hours of observing his immaculately sculpted body, was always the perfect bait.

"I don't like how close it's getting," Cynthia whispered as if the oversized fish could hear them. "It keeps moving so fast!"

Alberto secretly agreed, but kept up his charade. "He's just trying to get a better look at you, that's all. Barracudas rely on their short bursts of speed to catch their prey. In short distances, they can move up to twenty-seven miles per hour. Pretty remarkable, isn't it?"

His client seemed unimpressed, ignoring the question and asking, "How fast are *we* moving?"

Alberto paused before giving his response, taking a moment to consider whether he should reply truthfully or not. The real answer: nowhere near as fast as this barracuda was capable of moving. There was no way he and Ms. Reynard would be able to out swim this pursuing fish—but why on earth would that be necessary? Alberto silently scolded himself for being so paranoid, especially at his level of experience. Barracuda attacks on humans were entirely anecdotal, the result of rumors spread by novice divers and swimmers who misidentified smaller sharks.

Of course, their stories never involved a monstrous red torpedo with teeth like giant glass shards . . .

"The average diver swims about fifty feet per minute when moving at a leisurely pace."

"Well, could we increase our pace beyond leisurely, please?"

Alberto laughed. "Now, Ms. Reynard, there is absolutely no reason why we should feel the need to distance ourselves from our new friend here."

The guide's statement was proved wrong the moment the last word left his lips. A dark red blur shoved its way in between their floating bodies, rocking Alberto away in a backwards somersault. Even as he frantically kicked his legs to right himself, he registered Cynthia's cry as one not only of fright—but of pain.

"Cynthia!" Alberto hollered, craning his neck in all directions to locate the suddenly aggressive creature. He spotted it lurking once again behind them, having instantly retreated after its single strike attack.

Keeping an eye on the barracuda, Alberto swam to Cynthia's side and immediately noticed the hand that pressed firmly against the thigh of her left leg. Thin, dark tendrils of blood snaked their way between the woman's fingers, the cerulean water turning the liquid from deep red to near black.

"Oh my God!" Cynthia cried. "It bit me! The fucking thing actually bit me!"

Alberto swung an arm around his panicked client's shoulder and, as calmly as he could, removed her hand from the bleeding wound. It was then he saw the small, glittering object on her finger sparkling under the penetrating rays of the midday sun.

"I told you to take off all your jewelry on my boat!" Alberto shouted at the sight of the diamond ring. "This is why it bit you! It's easy for a barracuda to mistake shiny things for prey!"

"I'm sorry!" Cynthia bawled. "Is it bad?"

"Not at all," Alberto answered, completely telling the truth. The barracuda had only taken a curious nibble. The nature of its charge had been merely reconnaissance, rather than a full out assault.

The fish stared at them now, remaining idle as it seemed to assess the situation. Alberto found the animal's look of plotting logic to be fathoms beyond unnerving, but perhaps the close encounter had cleared up its confusion once and for all. It now knew that Cynthia was indeed not a fish, having nipped off the smallest of samples from her leg. But instead of losing interest in the huddling couple and wandering off in search of another food source, it remained lurking behind them—its strategy hidden behind soulless, black eyes.

"Give the ring to me." Alberto held out his right hand while keeping his eyes trained on the predator. Looking away from the glinting teeth that'd punctured her flesh, Cynthia removed the expensive ring from her finger and placed it in Alberto's palm. He transferred it to a zippered pouch on his belt.

"There," Alberto said, securing the jewelry, "Now how about we finally get to the cay?"

Before Cynthia could answer the loaded question, a streaking missile rushed across Alberto's peripheral vision with the speed of scarlet lightning. Alberto could only squeeze his eyes shut in the single second it took for the barracuda to commence its vicious attack.

Alberto opened his eyes, expecting to discover a bloody stump where his client's head should be. Instead, he found the woman seemingly unharmed, minus the small cut from before.

"Are you okay?" the guide yelled, motioning for her to feel all over herself for wounds.

"Yes," she answered without hesitation. "It didn't go after me this time."

"Then what—" Alberto's question trailed off when he tilted his eyes downward to see the gargantuan, red barracuda using its intimidating larger size to chase away several others of its fellow species. The expert guide could easily identify the smaller barracuda as the everyday, yellow-tail variety, or Sphyraena flavicauda. The big daddy darted at the smaller fish, gnashing its teeth and scattering the school in all directions. It was the behavior of any alpha male demonstrating its dominance—

—or claiming its food.

"Come on!" Alberto grabbed Cynthia's hand and yanked her away from the violent scene. They only had to make it two hundred feet to the cay. Maybe the yellow tail barracuda would buy the time they needed before the alpha male realized its lunch had gotten away.

Cynthia, of course, had become aware of Alberto's urgent tone and had resorted to pure hysterics and blubbering. Alberto ignored her frantic cries, kicking as hard as he could and ordering the bawling woman to do the same. He could feel the barracuda's presence behind them, a relentless murdering force of nature centimeters from their heels. Any moment now and the barracuda would rip his client from his hand

Any moment now . . .

A cloud of swirling sand erupted from below as his knee collided with something hard. At first, Alberto believed the object to be the barracuda, the sand to be the churning debris of Cynthia's insides. But after reaching a hand down and feeling the soft embrace of solid ground, he understood the fortunate truth.

They had reached the shallow waters surrounding the beach of the cay.

Alberto tore off his diving helmet, ripping the earpiece out in the process. It landed in a patch of muddy sand. He completely disregarded the gadget in order to hoist his exhausted client from the lapping tide and onto the beach. Cynthia lay at his feet, removing her own helmet as she struggled to catch her breath. After a minute of heavy gasping, Alberto extended a hand and assisted the woman to her feet.

"Now," Alberto said, brushing away a soaked lock of Cynthia's hair from her eyes, "wasn't that exciting?"

"Exciting?" Cynthia stepped backward, her eyes bulging. "I can't believe we got away! We almost got ripped to shreds by that whole school of barracuda!"

Alberto laughed. "*You* almost got ripped to shreds. I wasn't the one who brought along a shiny object to attract every carnivorous fish in the ocean." He paused, taking a moment to reach down and retrieve the large serrated diving knife strapped to his leg. "Well, except for this."

Cynthia nervously stared at the razor-sharp blade twirling in his hands. But what made her even more uneasy was the ominous aggression that had suddenly washed over her scuba guide's eyes.

"I guess you've got me there," Cynthia anxiously muttered, chuckling in an effort to conceal her growing fear. "You were probably right all along. It must have started following me because it thought I was a predator."

Alberto tilted his head, smiling. "No. My first guess was close, but I've figured it out now. It didn't think you were a predator—"

He snatched a handful of her long, wet hair and threw her to the sand.

"—it knew I was one."

Twenty minutes later, Alberto threw the body of Cynthia Reynard from a perfectly situated high cliff into the crashing waves below. Here, the water was deep enough to allow the gargantuan barracuda access to the floating carcass and to begin its well awaited binge. It only took three minutes for the fish to show up and prove Alberto's theories correct. The barracuda must have discovered Alberto's discarded victims and had acquired a new taste.

Alberto wiped his blood-stained knife with some damp palm fronds and used the blade to puncture a fallen coconut. As he sat in the shade of the tree, drinking sweet coconut milk and watching the barracuda enjoy its meal, he couldn't help but admire the animal's cleverness. Ms. Reynard had been the fifth woman vacationing by herself whom Alberto had seduced and taken to this secluded cay. And just like the rest, he'd forced her at knife point to hand over her hotel room key and the combination to the room's safe, as well as her ATM pin. Despite her cooperation, Alberto had then slashed her throat as he had the others, but not before offering one last bit of knowledge that a school of barracuda was actually called a *battery*.

"We make a good team," Alberto said to himself, mentally addressing the feeding fish. "I get the goods, you take care of the evidence." He took another swig from the coconut and added, "Even if you were a little impatient this time. Would've been a waste of an entire day if you'd snatched her before I got the info I needed."

With the last of the coconut milk drained, Alberto stood and brushed himself off. The setting sun was now halfway to the horizon, bringing to the sky a brilliant, reddish tinge. According to old sailor lore, the current conditions promised pleasurable weather tomorrow.

Alberto smiled. *The perfect weather for diving. But which lucky lady will it be?*

Reattaching his helmet, the pro diver prepared to depart before the overwhelming darkness arrived to make its daily claim on the night. After all his buckles and straps had been securely fastened, Alberto marched into the foaming water. He looked forward to going through the valuables Ms. Reynard had left on his boat.

Reaching the edge of the shallow water, Alberto felt the ocean's bottom drop out of reach from his feet when his left knee ignited in fiery pain. Alberto jerked his head around to see the red barracuda shooting away, a thin trail of blood in its wake. Frozen in utter surprise, Alberto watched the fish make a short, arching left and begin its return. Before he could even start to anticipate the predator's next move, the barracuda shot forward again, slicing Alberto's shoulder this time with its teeth.

"Gaah!" Alberto cried out, frantically kicking his right leg to propel himself away, backwards to the shallow water where the barracuda could not pursue. Fortunately, it only took the scuba diver mere seconds to regain his footing and return to safety. But he could still feel the heat of blood saturating his wetsuit, even warmer than the temperate ocean water. If he wanted to assess his injuries, Alberto had no choice but to walk back onto the shore.

He arrived at the hot, white sand of the cay's beach and once again ripped off his diving helmet. He turned to the ocean, trying to catch a glimpse of the barracuda's dorsal fin. How could it still be hungry? It had just devoured an entire human being. Even a fish that size couldn't stomach so much food at once.

The answer flashed before his mind's eye like an instantly loading web page: *Large barracudas, when gorged, may attempt to herd a school of prey fishes in shallow water, where they guard over them until they are ready for another meal.*

"You don't have to do this!" Alberto screamed at the ocean as if the barracuda could both hear and understand him. "I can bring you more food! Haven't you learned that? You eat me and there's no more! I—"

Alberto cut himself short when he realized the immense absurdity of his blabbering outburst. Deadly, instinctual hunters they may be, but barracudas were not rational thinkers. They were simply fish. And for all of Alberto's expertise, nothing would ever change that.

UNKINDLY GIRLS

Hailey Piper

ON THE THIRD MORNING AT Cherry Point, Morgan met the unkindly girls. Dawn had hardly touched the beach, giving the sand a grayish tone. Red rocks dotted the stone path from their small white beach house down to the water. Up the shore, a fishing boat cast off.

Morgan wore the ugliest swimsuit. Dad's decision—a one-piece, dull maroon abomination with sleeves and shorts. She'd never been allowed to wear a bikini, but in the past her swimsuits had looked presentable. The designer must've thought the faintest hint of shoulders and butt would draw too many wandering eyes.

Dad probably agreed. "You're still my baby girl," he'd said when Morgan complained. Six years old versus sixteen made little difference to him. He would scoff when he saw women and girls wear more revealing swimsuits. He'd call them unkindly—one of his favorite words, as if to look appealing meant flipping him off.

But Morgan had spent her life at his side and had seen him lick those chastising lips. She was not to become an unkindly girl. Never.

"You wouldn't do that to dear old Dad, Morgie," he'd say.

She'd come out early to dip into the water, but with so few people wandering the beach, she had her pick of seashells. The more colorful, the better. Hunting for them used to be a treat. Dad would only let her keep three per trip. He said to take too many would damage the ecosystem or something, but the hunt was the fun part.

Now, every shell that sparkled on the beach turned dull in her hands. She let them tumble back to the sand, one by one. A lot had changed at home since last summer. Try as she might to leave it behind, the change had followed her to Cherry Point.

"That is the ugliest thing I've ever seen."

Morgan dropped her last lackluster seashell and looked down the beach, where two girls her age walked the damp sand. One's face was all angles and wreathed in dark hair. The other flashed a soft smile; white stripes patterned her red hair where she'd bleached it. They wore dark, baggy pants and loose-fitting blouses that bared their chests.

Unkindly. The word popped unwanted into Morgan's head. She'd never glanced at other girls' chests the previous summers, but now Dad's eyes dominated hers.

"Like wearing blood," said the pointy-faced girl, still fixated on the swimsuit. "Sickening."

"Isn't it?" Morgan asked, tugging one stunted sleeve. "That's what the tag says. Ugliest Swimsuit, one size fits none."

The two girls giggled, and then the pointy-faced one beckoned Morgan. "I'm Blue, and the redhead's Clown. Follow us. We'll fix you up."

Morgan smiled to herself and obeyed. This wasn't unusual for summer vacation. Somehow, she always made at least one friend.

Neighbor houses squatted a couple hundred feet from each other, but closer to the wet sand stood a dull wooden shop. Water damage darkened its lower walls, and the discoloration gave the shop a sea-worn feel.

Blue and Clown led Morgan inside. Plastic shovels and pails dangled from nails, snorkels lined a metal tray, and bathing suits hung on a circular clothing rack. Plus, there were shelves of the usual gift shop garbage. A tacky ceramic crab clutching a flag in its claw read, "Ain't Life a Beach?"

The shopkeeper, a balding man with a scraggly goatee, let his eyes wander up and down the other girls' bodies. Morgan thought of Dad and how he'd never be so obvious. His shame always forced him to avert his gaze.

Fabric swatted her arm, tearing her gaze from the shopkeeper. Clown shook a plastic hanger, dangling an aquamarine two-piece swimsuit with navy-blue striping. Shiny sequins lay trapped between layers in the trim. They looked almost like scales and made Morgan think of mermaids.

"Lovely, yes?" Blue asked. Her smile was all teeth.

Morgan shrugged, but Blue was right. It was gorgeous.

Blue guided the bikini to Morgan's front. "On you. To die for, yes?"

Exactly Morgan's thinking. Dad would kill her.

Morgan stepped back, letting the two-piece dangle again. "It's pretty, but I don't have money."

"We'll spot you," Blue said, taking the hanger from Clown. "In return, you hang with us tonight on the beach. Agreed?"

Morgan shrank inside. If only it weren't so easy to make friends, Dad would have no one to chastise, and these would be peaceful vacations, nothing more.

Blue laid the swimsuit on the counter. The shopkeeper didn't look at her now, his eyes sharply focused on the cash register. Clown reached inside her blouse and pulled out a black purse. Dollar coins thudded on the checkout counter. Morgan couldn't see their faces, but they made her think of pirate doubloons.

Blue pressed the swimsuit into Morgan's arms. "At the beach, just before sunset." She marched past, and Clown trailed her.

Morgan began to follow them out.

The shopkeeper cleared his throat. "Watch out for them two."

Morgan turned to him. "What?"

He ran his fingernails from temple to goatee, scratching an itch he couldn't catch. "Every summer, they come to Cherry Point and sell dope up and down the beach. Don't get caught in their mess." He began to fiddle with a coin, but his eyes focused on Blue and Clown as they sauntered out the door.

Vacationers, not locals.

They were just the kind of girls who'd make Dad avert his eyes.

If they would stop going to the beach each summer, maybe he wouldn't have to see any unkindly girls. Sometimes he saw them at the pool in Syracuse, but nothing would come of that. Too close to home.

When Morgan was little, she'd thought their beach trips were a fun way to spend each summer together after Mom died. Cape Cod, Miami Beach, La Jolla. Different coasts, different kinds of beaches, but always full of sand castles, ice cream, and splashing in the shallows, though ever past the sea shelf where the undertow might suck her into the deep. Safety first was one of Dad's rules.

At each beach, Morgan made a friend. She never meant to. They would stumble into each other, or Morgan would see the other girl wearing something pretty. A day would pass, Dad would disappear for a night, and then they would head home.

Morgan tiptoed through the beach house and into her room, where she stashed the aquamarine bikini beneath her sagging mattress. Cool salty air swept through an open window and across her arms. She stripped out of her maroon one-piece and dressed in a tank and shorts. She'd meant to swim, but now a grimmer outlook haunted her thoughts.

She would have to tell Dad about the girls. Since Mom was gone, she'd told him everything, even after she realized he hadn't been telling her everything in return.

Utensils clinked in the kitchen. He was awake.

She stared at her window, thinking about sneaking out, but Cherry Point lay hundreds of miles from Syracuse. If she ran away, she'd just have to come back. He would think her unkindly for worrying him, and he might then worry that she knew his secret.

She traipsed into the kitchen. Dad loomed over the stovetop, his thick yet dexterous fingers sliding an egg from bowl to rim to pan. He wore a blue and white Hawaiian pattern shirt, khaki shorts, and white sandals. Harmless middle-class vacation father—his best costume.

"Morning, Morgie," he said. "Out early?"

"I wanted to swim while it was cool," she said, plopping down on a stool by the kitchen island. The pedestal creaked around a loose screw.

"Your hair's dry." Dad didn't look at her. Somehow he just knew these things. Another egg cracked and sizzled.

"I didn't get a chance. I made a friend."

Dad focused hard on his hands as he slid his graceful spatula beneath the omelet. It flipped and hissed against the pan. "That's nice."

"A couple friends, actually." The cold marble countertop felt soothing under Morgan's palms. If she kept them there, could she keep from getting blood on her hands?

Dad picked up a knife. Its blade slid around the omelet, sawing off brown arms of crust. "Staying safe, right?" he asked, working magic with pepper and cheese. "Staying kindly?"

Dad laid a plate on the countertop. The omelet was perfect, all signs of burning and crust cut close as could be without losing any of the cheesy yellow center.

Morgan swallowed before biting. "Yes, Daddy. Always."

He would watch her leave tonight. He would see Blue and Clown, and then lick his chastising lips.

Morgan didn't say goodbye in the evening. They wouldn't really be apart, after all, though only she would approach the beach, where the unkindly girls sat around a small fire just outside the tide's reach. Coastal winds batted at the flames. A storm was coming.

"Now what are you wearing?" Blue asked. She and Clown had not changed out of loose-fitting blouses.

Morgan wore baggy jeans and a hoodie. She'd told Dad that it was going to be chilly this close to the water tonight.

"Where's your swimsuit?"

"Under my clothes, same as yours," Morgan said. The girls tittered, and she realized their cleavage was still on display, no hint of bikini tops underneath.

Clown tugged a large brown bottle from the sand beside her feet, took a swig, and passed it around the fire, first to Blue and then to Morgan. There was no label. Brine clung to the bottom, as if the glass had been trapped in a shipwreck for a hundred years.

She thought of Dad and passed the bottle back to Clown. "Anything fresher?"

"We'll have something fresher after sunset," Blue said. She and Clown tittered again, the only sound Clown seemed to make. Her hair caught the firelight; its shadows twitched this way and that, as if alive.

As red and purple dusk gave way to black, cloud-covered night, the small fire became an island of light on the beach. Windows glowed down the beach, except at Morgan's house, but the rest of the world was dark. She wondered exactly where Dad was holed up. He could be anywhere the light didn't touch while the campfire illuminated the girls for him.

She'd figured things out after last summer. It wasn't like in the movies where he might've accidentally left out some crucial clue that grabbed her attention or a serendipitous news article happened to link their past vacation locales. She was older now and getting attention from boys at school. The way they looked at her wasn't so different from her father. They were just too juvenile to feel shame. Then there were his comments, his averted eyes, and the nights he'd go out before they left their vacation spots for home. Her brain had linked the chains.

Now she wrapped those chains around her legs. She wondered what heavy thing she'd tether them to and throw into the ocean to drag her down.

"The night's ready, girls," Blue said, standing up and turning to Morgan. "Fancy a swim?" She didn't wait for an answer, just tromped toward the water and expected the others to follow.

They did. Where the tide lapped at their feet, Clown spun around and held out a fist to Morgan. She took the offering, a coarse square that reminded her of dehydrated fruit.

"Ever been swimming high?" Blue asked. "Unforgettable."

And unkindly. Morgan made to pass the square back, but Clown was already running into the tide.

The light was gone. Dad would never know, same as he'd never know about the sequined bikini. Morgan lifted her palm to her mouth, and her lips closed around the square.

"Melts on your tongue," Blue said. She was already knee-deep, the tide drenching her clothes.

Morgan stripped and followed. Salt spray stung her nose. Her mouth filled with the static that blew from Dad's radio when he let her switch between stations. The other girls bobbed, dark driftwood on black waves.

Vague warnings slid beneath Morgan's thoughts. "The shelf. The undertow."

Thunder and waves drowned her out. The girls drifted farther. Morgan meant to follow. Only the thought of Dad anchored her to land. She wasn't an unkindly girl. Never.

Waves rolled toward her. She took a deep breath, stinking of seawater, and plunged beneath the surface. She couldn't see underneath, but somehow she knew that Blue and Clown were diving, too. The ocean became less an undulating wave, more a hand that grabbed Morgan and yanked her deep.

She floated beneath the creaking hull of an aging ship, its underside as glassy and coated in barnacles as the bottle passed between Blue and Clown. Inside, pirates dragged helpless hook hands against smooth walls. Their glass prison was filled with seawater and beer, and their pockets were so loaded with doubloons that they couldn't swim away.

Blue and Clown beckoned Morgan to the surface, their scaly

50

turquoise and orange tails flapping. Neither mermaid seemed unkindly. They just wanted to see selfish men die.

An enormous golden tail rocked the drowning ship. The black sky flickered alive with lightning, painting the silhouette of an enormous woman against the clouds. If Blue and Clown were guppies, she was a shark. Plains of kelp matted her scaly head, and coral coated her arms. One gargantuan hand grabbed the bottle by the neck and slung it at the sky. It shattered in thunder, and its shards sliced every pirate to pieces. Their lungs flopped atop the water's surface, helpless as fish on land.

"Unforgettable," Blue said.

Morgan dug her hands into wet sand and hauled herself onto the beach. The tide splashed across her back, spraying saltwater into her mouth, but her muscles felt too worn to move another inch. Rain pattered the sand. The storm that swirled out on the water had almost reached Cherry Point. Whatever drug Clown had given to Morgan, it seemed to be losing its effect.

Lightning forked overhead, illuminating a smoking mound where the campfire once burned. Morgan thought she saw other shapes closer to the water. She stared hard at black on black outlines until the sky lit in another blue flicker.

Two naked bodies lay in the surf, red and white hair swirled around one's head. A bulky figure kneeled beside them. The flicker faded as he turned to Morgan, and he stared until lightning again tore across the sky. Its flash lit his familiar eyes and made his chastising lips glisten.

"I'm sorry, Morgie, but they were unkindly," Dad said. Thunder rumbled, and he paused for it to pass. "You know, don't you? I thought you knew when you told me about them." He started toward her.

Morgan's chest ached against the sand. She wanted to slither back into the water. She felt the lightning coming, the sky's tattling forked tongue, and the beach glowed as blue as her swimsuit. He could see her clear as day.

She lifted her head. "Dad—"

"What are you wearing, Morgie?" he asked, but he didn't say it like a question. He sounded the same as when she was six, the day he told her Mom wasn't coming home. Thoughts of him had shriveled out on the water, but now he was here and real, and he dwarfed every fantastical ocean.

"I-I-I—" Morgan tried to stand, but her legs felt waterlogged. She wondered if that was the drug's doing. She managed to sit up and wrap her gooseflesh-covered arms around her chest.

"It was only a matter of time, wasn't it?" He sounded calm, almost peaceful. He squatted down, drew her into his firm arms, and scooped her up against his chest. Fire beat inside in time to the spitting rain. "You had to grow up someday."

Morgan closed her eyes and tried to forget everything she'd realized since last summer. Dad used to be a good man, or at least that's what she'd believed. She could believe it again, couldn't she? If he just held her like this and warmed her bones against every chilly seaborne wind, she would believe anything he wanted.

"Daddy, carry me home," she said. Lightning flickered past her eyelids. "It can be like it was." She felt him walking, but he hadn't turned around.

"It can't," he said.

Water slopped at her dangling feet. She opened her eyes. The world lay dark between lightning flickers, but she made out frothing waves that encircled them, churned ugly by harsh wind. Dad was walking into the sea.

"Why?" she asked.

"Because I can't feel the way I feel about unkindly girls for you!" he shouted, loud as thunder. "Not my baby girl. Never."

She squirmed, but she'd exhausted herself, and he held her tight. Rain and sea crashed across her, plastering her swimsuit against her skin. He didn't look at her, averting his eyes for when lightning next lit the coast.

He didn't have to avert them for long. Chest-deep in the water, he plunged her under. One hand grasped her shoulder; the other shoved hard against her head. She clawed at his unyielding wrists and kicked at his legs and groin, but her feet were heavy, the water weighing them down. Lightning reflected in Dad's eyes. The storm would watch her die.

Was this how he'd killed the other girls, every summer vacation past? Had he held them first so that they might know a loving embrace before drowning them? Always far from home, those unkindly girls. They were vacationers who might've met anyone on the beach, but instead they'd met Morgan and her father. Dead summer friends were coming to collect. She had been his accomplice, knowing or not, and she would join them beneath the sea. He hadn't been caught for murdering them; would someone wonder why he returned to Syracuse alone this time? Would neighbors ask if Morgan died kindly?

He would tell them so. Someone would come to collect him, and he'd say his daughter died still his baby girl. Always.

Morgan stopped fighting. Her lungs screamed to keep thrashing, but she had to catch his gaze. She stared up at him, bubbles slipping from her lips. The sea calmed for a moment, as if anticipating a mighty wave. Dad glanced down at her.

Lightning flashed. She slipped her fingers beneath the lower rim of her bikini top and yanked it up.

Had he waited, the lightning would have faded and he wouldn't have seen, but even a glimpse seemed too much. His body shuddered backward. He turned his head, eyelids squeezed shut, the sight threatening to drive nails through his eyeballs.

The tide crashed across them, shoving him back and taking her under. It bought her time to break from the shallows. She dove under the next wave. Thunder crashed, but it came warped and uncertain underwater. She thought she might be swimming over the sea shelf by now. Her skin stung with cold as she surfaced.

"Morgie!"

Dad swam against the waves. His drenched clothing tugged at him, but she'd been fighting the ocean for an unknown time, whereas he had a fresh start. He could manage. His fingers snatched her ankle.

If he tried to drown her this far from shore, he'd probably kill them both. Would keeping her kindly be worth the sacrifice?

She looked out to sea for the miracle she'd seen earlier, but there was no static in her mouth, only her tongue. The drug had worn off. No mermaid was coming to save her, same as no one had saved her summer friends in every year past.

She let Dad draw her close and wrapped both arms around his trunk. He embraced her, too. He might've thought she was trying to hug him, one last desperate grasp for sympathy.

She sucked in a deep breath and thrust downward hard as she could. Flexing her legs, she kicked herself and Dad into the next wave, where the undertow pulled them under. He was stronger and larger, but freed of land, she could move him.

He shoved at her face. Lightning revealed his flailing limbs—he must've missed the chance to take a breath before submerging.

She didn't let go. Her lungs burned again, still faint from the first attempted drowning. She promised them this would be the last.

Fighting him wasn't just about Blue and Clown. It was about all the unkindly girls he had already killed and all the ones who might die yet. No more.

Burning faded from her chest, her lungs at last giving out. The surface seemed far away, and she was tired. Ghostly cold ate through her muscles. One more unkindly girl drowned in the deep.

Lightning burned in ferocious flashes, the sky playing catch between two clouds, and the world flickered black and blue. An ocean of fish and seaweed appeared. Vanished. Returned full of faces. Morgan might've believed they belonged to mermaids or dead pirates, but when the next lightning flash brought them closer, she recognized them.

They were easy to remember; none had aged since she'd last seen them. Little girls, adolescents, teens, Blue and Clown among them. All her summer friends.

And there were strangers who crowded beyond, more than Dad should've murdered in the ten years he'd been taking Morgan on summer vacation, more unkindly girls than years in her life. Some were women who might've been Mom's age. Others he must've met when he was younger.

He had been finding unkindly girls for a long time. Noticing them and averting his gaze, he poured his strength into unlatching Morgan's legs. He didn't seem to realize she was dead.

The ocean formed hands in the uncertain darkness between lightning flashes. They hugged him, hugged her. The undertow, the dead—she couldn't tell what helped her hold him anymore. The difference mattered little to a ghost. No more breathing, eating, or sleeping. No more distracting life functions. She could focus now, all secrets bare, and bend her will to one purpose.

The dead wanted him, and she wouldn't let go.

DEEP IN THE HEART

Waylon Jordan

WE PULLED INTO THE PARKING lot at the Heart of Texas Caverns and spilled out of the vehicle into the humid heat of a Texas July.

My mom and dad were beyond ready for this vacation to be over, but they had finally relented to one more stop on the road home after I, in what had passed for subtlety in my twelve-year-old brain, had read aloud every cave tour billboard I had seen for the last two hundred miles.

The gravel crunched beneath my feet and the drone of cicadas in the trees and fields around us filled my ears. The heat and humidity turned the air to hot soup and in under a minute, my hair was already sticking to my forehead. A light breeze would have been a blessing.

We arrived just in time for the next tour. Dad purchased our passes and pushed us toward a small group of maybe thirteen people near the cog train that would take us down into the cave.

Our tour guide had shaggy brown hair, blue eyes and a mouth full of perfectly straight, white teeth. He had on tight khaki shorts and an equally tight green polo embroidered with the Heart of Texas Caverns emblem.

At twelve years old and raised in deep East Texas, I didn't yet have the courage nor the vocabulary to say that I was gay. I didn't even fully know what that meant, but I knew that I was absolutely fascinated by the dark brown hair on his toned legs and the patch of skin visible near his unbuttoned shirt collar. I was more than a little embarrassed when I realized he caught me looking. Thankfully, my parents didn't notice.

"Hey, everyone!" he called, pulling everyone else's attention to him. He obviously had mine already. "My name is Danny. I'm nineteen years old, a Freshman at Stephen F. Austin State University, and I'll be taking you Deep in the Heart of Texas Caverns today!"

He sang the "Deep in the Heart of Texas" line and was rewarded with a few chuckles from his captive audience.

"I'm going to ask all of you to stick close to the group while we're down there. There are parts of these caverns that have never been explored and I don't get paid to play Magellan!"

"Next I'm going to ask you to remember not to touch anything while we're down there. A cavern system is a living, breathing ecosystem. We're visitors in their house and the oils on our hands can kill pieces of formations that have stood for centuries."

He looked at the kids in the group and grinned.

"If you think your mom gets mad when you put your hands all over her clean windows, she's got nothing on my boss. So do a fella a favor and try to remember, okay? Alright, onto the train everyone! Aaaalll aboard!"

We loaded onto the train and Danny made his way to the front where he picked up a handheld mic that would amplify his voice while we descended.

The train made a distinct sound when it rumbled to life. It reminded me of the mini roller coaster at our local county fair back home. My excitement grew as we left the surface world behind and headed into the cave's dark depths.

"When we get to the end of the line, we'll be about one hundred and forty feet below the surface," Danny said. "Honestly, spaces like this used to give me the creeps. I didn't want to take this job, but I finally caved!"

Danny was again rewarded with a few chuckles from his audience, but I just smiled and looked at my feet. It's not that I didn't think Danny's jokes were funny. It's just that every time he told one, he would flash that grin again.

That grin put rabbit-sized butterflies in my stomach and I could not afford to let my parents see me squirm.

"If you look to your left, you'll be able to see your first stalagmites and stalactites. Does anyone know the difference?"

He waited a few seconds and when no one volunteered to answer, he just shook his head.

"Oh boy. Everyone has to go back to earth science class," he joked. "Stalagmites and stalactites are mineral formations. Stalagmites grow up from the cave floor and stalactites grow down from the ceiling. They've got a lot in common with ants in the pants, actually. When the mites go up, the tights come down!"

His audience groaned, but I leaned around my dad to see what Danny was talking about.

I had always pictured stalagmites and stalactites as dry, gray rock, but these weren't like that at all. They were brown, gold, and beige. Every shade in between and their damp surfaces shimmered in the lights set up along the tracks.

As we descended deeper, the train's movements echoed unpleasantly. Danny continued to talk, but even with the mic's amplification, parts of the tour were garbled. I wondered if we'd missed any of his endearingly corny jokes in the noise.

Finally, the train eased to a halt and I was relieved the sound, which had nearly become unbearable, died away. Danny motioned us off the train.

My dad huddled us together into a group and we were soon walking along the stone floor of the remarkably well-lit cave. I was immediately struck by how cool the temperature was here.

Danny pointed out natural formations that bore striking resemblances to horses, birds, people, and even bacon strips, which made me smile. Next, he led us through a tunnel with colorful, crystal-lined walls. I stopped to look at them, completely missing the fact the tour had moved on without me.

Earlier in the year, I had read *The Crystal Cave* by Mary Stewart. In the book, Merlin discovered a cave whose walls were lined with smooth crystals. I had spent hours trying to imagine what it might have looked like. I thought I had a pretty good idea, but this was so much better. It was like standing in a fairy tale.

I stood there, turning in circles, watching the way the crystals winked at me in yellows, reds, and blues until I heard a strange noise. It sounded like something was sliding roughly across the stone floor of the cave interrupted by a single, rhythmic slapping sound.

Slide, slap, slide slap, slide slap.

I looked back. The tunnel was so brightly lit, a contrast to the entrance, that it was hard to see anything beyond its threshold. I jumped when a hand suddenly fell on my shoulder.

"Hey, guy, no falling behind," Danny said, smiling at me.

"I thought I heard something."

"Yeah, there's all kinds of weird noises down here, but you gotta keep up. Come on," he said, turning me around and walking me back to rejoin the group. His hand was warm on my shoulder and the butterflies immediately returned to my stomach with a fury.

I did not want him to move his hand. I also didn't want him to *know* that I didn't want him to move his hand, and I could feel my face burning as we caught sight of the tour group standing together trying not to look bored.

My dad was shooting daggers, but he didn't say anything. I knew I'd be in for it when the tour ended.

Danny, however, never missed a beat. He led us to a pool where catfish swam. He explained the fish had lived in the cave system for so many generations that they no longer had eyes.

"Use it or lose it," Danny joked and winked at me when I was the only one who laughed. "But seriously, nature is resourceful. It loses what it doesn't need and develops what it does."

"What do they eat?" someone in the group asked.

"Smaller fish. Bugs. I've heard they'll even eat bats if they get too close to the water, but don't quote me on it."

A shiver went down my spine at Danny's explanation and I immediately stepped back from the edge of the water. My dad loved to fish and he loved to make me go with him. I knew that larger fish would eat smaller fish and worms, but it had never occurred to me that they might eat animals outside of the water.

I had felt the gritty, sharp inside of a catfish's mouth before and my mind immediately went to work imagining one of them closing around my arm trying to devour me.

"No thanks," I whispered and took another step back.

After a while, Danny brought us to a halt inside a large round chamber and I looked up into its craggy ceiling. Something didn't feel right here. There were multiple openings aside from the one we had entered but they had no lighting in them and I couldn't shake the feeling that someone or something could be watching us from the dark. I stepped closer to my mom as the hair stood up on the back of my neck and goosebumps broke out along my arms.

"People talk about being afraid of the dark, but most people don't know what real darkness is," Danny began. "Even on a moonless night, there is still starlight. Even when all the lights are turned off in our houses, the VCR clock still shines."

I had never really considered it before, but he was right. There were always streetlights, car headlights and any number of illumination sources no matter what time of night it was.

"Total darkness is unsettling," Danny continued. "It's uncomfortable."

My stomach churned as he dug into his shirt pocket and removed a tiny birthday candle.

"In total darkness, the flame on this candle would be an astonishing amount of light," he said. "Now, I need a volunteer to help me with a little experiment."

He made a big show of walking around the chamber, smiling at everyone individually, but ultimately he stopped in front of me.

"How about you?" he asked.

My mouth was dry and I found it difficult to answer, but I felt a push from behind as my dad volunteered me. Danny put his hand on my shoulder again and walked me to the other side of the chamber where an almost cartoonishly large switch was attached to the wall.

"What's your name?"

"Michael," I whispered, then cleared my throat. "My name is Michael."

"Okay, Michael. Don't worry. This is going to be easy."

He winked at me before he turned back to the rest of our tour group. The attention made me blush, and blushing made me blush more.

"Okay everyone, for your safety, I'm going to ask you to back up close to the walls. In just about a minute here, my new buddy, Michael, is going to pull this switch. When he does, you're going to experience total darkness for the very first time! Please, no matter what your first instincts are, stay close to the wall. You don't know how many people I've had try to run and end up falling. Everyone understand?"

They all looked so excited, and they whispered to each other as they arranged themselves in front of the wall opposite Danny and me. One man picked up his daughter, who looked like she might have been only six or seven, and whispered to her. She giggled and clapped her hands.

"Lights out!" she shouted and clapped some more.

My mom had a firm grip on my dad, who was grinning at me.

My father wasn't a cruel man, but he definitely thought I was too soft. I spent too much time reading and not enough time hunting, fishing, and exploring the outdoors "being a boy," as he put it, so anything that pushed me outside my comfort zone was just fine by him.

"All right, Michael," Danny said. "I'm going to count down from three and when I get to one, I want you to pull that switch, okay? I'm going to be right here and when I tell you, just push it back up to turn the lights back on. Got it?"

"Yeah. I mean, yes, sir."

"Don't call me 'sir,' buddy," he said, grinning. "I'm not nearly old enough for that. Yet. Okay, is everyone ready?"

Everyone on the opposite wall answered in the affirmative and Danny stepped to my side, putting his hand on my shoulder again.

"All right! Lights out in three, two, one . . . "

Nervously, I pulled down on the switch. As the lights fell away, I was almost certain I saw *something* step into the chamber.

Everything was quiet for maybe three or four seconds aside from the "ohs" and "ahs" from the rest of the tour group.

"I can't see my hand in front of my own face!" someone yelled.

"This is so cool," someone else said, laughing nervously.

Danny's hand was still firmly on my shoulder and I leaned into his grip just a bit in an attempt to reassure myself that I wasn't alone. I had never been afraid of the dark, but I had never liked it either.

This? This was something completely different.

No matter how well Danny had explained it, there was simply no way of anticipating how disorienting total darkness would be. My stomach flipped with anxiety as I realized I no longer had a way of navigating this environment. I could have been upside down standing on the ceiling and it wouldn't surprise me for a second.

Thank God for Danny's hand. It felt like an anchor holding me steady.

That's when I heard that strange sound again. It sounded like someone sliding their feet across the stone floor of the cave but always with the slap that followed the slide.

Slide, slap, slide, slap, slide slap.

"Stay against the wall," Danny called, but the shuffling steps continued.

I said a silent prayer but my thoughts derailed when the total darkness was shattered by a strange tearing sound and an ear-splitting scream that lasted maybe two or three seconds before cutting off abruptly as something fell to the floor.

From the time I was just a little kid, if I became completely overwhelmed or scared, I would shut down. My muscles would tense; my joints would lock. I became completely useless until I felt whatever danger I perceived had passed.

The sudden silence was far more terrifying than the scream itself, and I fell into that familiar trancelike state, my hand locking onto the switch as my body went rigid with fear.

"Okay, Michael, time to turn the light back on."

Danny's voice sounded like it was miles away. I *wanted* to turn the lights back on, but I couldn't.

"Michael, turn on the light!"

This time it was my mom's voice and it managed to cut through the haze that had fallen around me, but not enough to make me move.

"What the fuck is that?"

I didn't recognize the voice.

"Let go of my leg or I'll shoot!"

Seconds later, I heard a man scream and the deafening sound of a handgun being fired as the muzzle flared and a bullet ricocheted. I heard Danny grunt and fall.

My anchor was gone and reality locked back into place. I needed the light and I needed it urgently.

A blaze of light filled the room as I slammed the switch back up again.

I immediately shielded my eyes and turned my head away from the glow of the artificial lights. My eyelids reflexively fluttered as the cave around me went from stark shades of black and white to color that was almost too vibrant.

As my vision cleared, I faced forward again where I could just make out the shape of the *thing* that had infiltrated our group.

It wasn't particularly tall, and its green-gray skin was shiny and sleek and wet. The creature was really no more than a torso and head with long arms that extended out in front of its distended belly. Its short, squat legs and long feet explained the strange sliding footsteps I'd heard earlier.

Two nasty horns grew from the place where the thing's eyes should have been. There were small slits in the skin I assumed served as its ears and nose. Most of the creature's face was occupied by a lipless and whiskered mouth, which currently chewed on a tourist's arm.

My thoughts flashed back to the pool and Danny's explanation of the strange catfish that lived in its dark and terrifying depths and how they would eat anything that got close enough to their pool.

Nature is resourceful.

No one moved or made a sound as we all took in the horror in front of us.

The creature sucked and spit as its creaking jaws chewed through muscle and bone. Loud gulps issued from its throat as it swallowed before it sucked the last of the arm into its mouth. I could hear the bones crack and break before the sucking and gulping sounds started again. Red-tinged saliva and bits of flesh, including a single finger with a simple gold band, dropped from the thing's mouth.

My stomach flipped and I knew I was moments away from vomiting if I didn't look away.

My eyes dropped to the creature's feet and I saw a woman lying there. If she wasn't dead already, she was well on her way. Her arm had been ripped off, blood steadily pooling around her. Her own finger now sat in the blood pointing to where her arm had been. The color looked almost pretty in the light.

The creature audibly swallowed what was left of the woman's arm, then opened its mouth and emitted a strange croaking sound. Seconds later, I heard shuffling in the shadows, and I realized it had announced the buffet was open.

Chaos broke out in the room as everyone ran in different directions. My dad was pushing my mom ahead of him. They headed toward one of the three exits and completely forgot about me.

To my left, I heard Danny cry out and I turned to see one of the creatures leaning over him, its hungry mouth open and dripping brackish saliva onto his face. I quickly realized he had been hit in the shoulder by the ricocheting bullet. The smell of the blood had no doubt drawn the creature directly to him.

"Run!" Danny shouted, looking me right in the eye. "Go back the way we came!"

His words turned to a scream as the creature ripped off a handful of his hair. It cooed with delight as it licked at the hair and reached out to grab Danny's one unwounded arm.

I don't know what came over me. Maybe it was because he was

nice to me. Maybe it was because he was cute. All I knew was I couldn't let this thing have him.

"Get back!" I shouted and leapt forward. I grabbed the heavy flashlight that hung from Danny's belt and wrestled it free.

The creature barely registered my presence until I brought the flashlight down on its head. The resulting squish turned my stomach. Its angry roar in response sent me stumbling backward, and I landed on Danny.

"I'm sorry, I'm sorry," I said, scrambling back to my feet. The creature held its head where green-black blood trickled from the fresh wound I'd created. It swiped at me wildly with its other clawed hand.

"Michael, just get out of here!" Danny shouted as he tried to scramble out from under the creature.

"I'm not leaving without you," I yelled back, then ran at the creature with arms raised, screaming at the top of my lungs. I felt the tips of its fingers swipe at my shirt as I brought the flashlight down again on its bulbous head. There was another disgusting squish that ended in a loud crack.

It was the creature's turn to stumble this time. Its short legs and elongated feet tangled together, sending it falling onto its back. Danny had finally managed to pull himself to his feet and I closed the distance between us, trying to catch my breath.

At the sound of that strange grunting, Danny and I turned to find the creature back on its feet. Danny grabbed me, pushing me behind him while simultaneously taking the flashlight from my hand. His roars matched those of the creature in front of him as he slammed the heavy metal light into the side of the thing's head.

It stumbled to the left and Danny hit it again. This time, when it fell, he leapt on top and brought the light down over and over again until its head was completely dented. Finally, the mysterious cave creature was dead.

Danny's face was streaked with the creature's blood when he stood and turned back to the room, his face a mixture of fear and rage.

He grabbed my hand and pulled me into the tunnel beyond the chamber's opening.

The path ahead was a blur as Danny pulled me along behind him, but he never let go. He held my hand until we were back in the sunlight and both of us stumbled to our knees gasping for air.

I leaned against him, not caring who saw or what it looked like.

Danny put his arm around me protectively.

People were shouting. It looked like at least a few members of our tour group had made it out ahead of us. The man who had picked up his daughter before the lights went out clutched her tightly in his arms as he yelled at what I assumed was Danny's boss.

There were others who must have been waiting for the next tour. They quickly backed away when they saw us. More than one ran for the parking lot and I heard tires screech as they sped away.

"Michael!" My mother called my name as she, too, went to her knees next to me, pulling me into her arms and kissing my face. "Are you okay? Did it hurt you?"

"I—I think I'm all right, mama," I whispered.

She scrambled by me and grabbed Danny, pulling him into her arms as well, thanking him for saving my life.

He winced as his wounded shoulder was jostled, but he managed to smile at her and look over at me.

"He saved mine first."

People from the ticket booth and the gift shop ran over to see what was happening, and I heard someone tell someone else to call the police. They pulled us inside and a skinny older man in a "Heart of Texas Caverns" shirt gave me one just like it so I could change.

By the time the police and ambulances had arrived, we were almost all cleaned up except Danny. One of his co-workers had removed his shirt and held a towel tightly to the gunshot wound in Danny's shoulder. The bald spot where the creature had ripped the hair from his head would have been comical if there weren't quite so much dried blood.

I joined my Mom and Dad, who were sitting nearby and my mom put her arm around me.

No one spoke. We just sat there as a family waiting for our turn to talk to the police.

I tried not to look at the cave, but I couldn't help it. Over and over again, my eyes were drawn to the entrance and the dark beyond it, and sometimes, I could swear I saw something moving.

What were those things?

No matter what my mind gave me as an explanation, nothing fit. They were monsters. Monsters were real.

Before, that entrance had seemed like a doorway to an adventure. Now, I couldn't shake the feeling that it was an open mouth waiting to be fed.

PEELINGS
Kenzie Jennings

THURSDAY, ITINERARY: PICK UP CAR *at Avis. Hotel check-in. Rest (girls at pool?). Dinner at Kyoto Hibachi.*

"Happiest place on earth needs a cheaper, happier hotel," Marc groused as he hung up the damp towels on the ironing board Beth had set out as a makeshift drying rack. "We're still a shuttle ride away from the park, and yet we're paying a month's worth of mortgage to stay three goddamn nights. That's some grade-A bullshit right there."

"You need to keep that language to a minimum. I already told you it was the only one I could find on short notice."

"Christ, Beth! How long were you out there? Your back."

By then, Marc had already joined her in the suite's narrow bathroom, his face furrowed in disgust. She looked over her shoulder at her reflection to see for herself.

He wasn't wrong. There was a stark contrast between the milky white cut-out patterns where her swimsuit had covered and the wide, fiery strips where it looked like blood had boiled beneath her skin. Marc pulled a little bottle of aloe from his Dopp kit, popped the snap lid, and squeezed some on his hand, his face bunched as he did.

Beth didn't want to hear it, but it was inevitable nonetheless. The chiding, the deep sighs wholly exaggerated for her benefit. It was all about treating her as if she were a child, like she was one of the twins, completely naïve to the big, bad strangeness of the world, and with

Marc there to guide her through the rough terrain.

No, that wasn't correct. The twins were treated better.

Beth caught snippets of the girls' whispers, punctuated by their shrieks and giggles over whatever it was they were watching on their iPad. It was probably some other unsuitable series on Netflix that Marc had brushed off as unimportant. Small favor that they'd brought the thing, Beth supposed, as it had kept the twins occupied during the flight, but it was infuriating that Marc had turned off the parental controls without conferring with her. "They're practically teenagers. I mean, they're going to be curious anyway, so we may as well let them check out things for themselves. It's not like everyone else is gonna censor anything around them," Marc had said in that tone he normally reserved for his younger staff, and, as of late, for Beth as well.

The coolness of the gel, combined with the warmth of Marc's hands, ought to have been soothing, but it felt abrasive, like he was attempting to rub the unsightly sunburn away. Anything to rid her of another flaw.

"Next time, get in the shade or something. Put up one of those umbrellas they set out," Marc said, punctuating with the snap of the bottle lid. "You can wear a tee over it tomorrow, cover it up."

"A tee won't let my skin breathe."

"Let your skin 'breathe'? What is that? Some dermatologist in a magazine make that up? Skin doesn't 'breathe'. That's stupid. Just cover it up so no one will see it. Gotta blend in or you're gonna look like a tourist."

"We *are* tourists," Beth snapped.

Marc turned her around, his fingers tightly grasping her chin. She flinched, tried to pull away, but he held her in close, his eyes narrowed. "You making it hard on me here, Beth?"

"Daddy, you doing okay?" Sadie called out from the bedroom. Of the twins, she was the one who was quick to come to Marc's defense no matter the issue, and it had grown from adorable to creepy over the years. By the time Sadie was deep in her teens, it wouldn't surprise Beth if she got a "daddy's girl" tattoo someplace entirely inappropriate.

"Daddy's just fine, sweetheart," he said over his shoulder, his eyes still locked with Beth's. "You girls need to get ready for dinner. Put on something nice, okay? We're going out for hibachi." He let go of Beth's chin, gave her a quick peck on the forehead, and murmured,

"Cover it up, baby. Trust me here. Wear that short, black thing you brought, the one with the sleeves and tie in front. Show those legs of yours."

"Oh, so no skin, but the legs are okay because legs don't have skin."

"You don't have to be a bitch about it. It's just a suggestion."

Well, it was always . . . *always* . . . "just a suggestion."

Friday, ITINERARY: Main park all day. Bring carryall. Get bottled water at park. Lunch there. Keep budget to a minimum (dinner, takeout?). SUN-SCREEN, you idiot!

It was the sixth queue of the day and, unfortunately, the longest. Still, anything to make the twins happy, something they could share on Snapchat and Instagram and whatever other horrible social networking site they had profiles on (Beth had lost that fight a long time ago). They'd predictably pouted and whined when Beth had them put their phones in one of the park's locker stations. Of course, when Marc had pointed out the practicality in it—that their phones could fall or even, perhaps, kill someone standing below—they stopped complaining and linked arms with his as they all headed for the line.

They'd been there moving in line at a snail's pace for roughly thirty minutes when Beth felt the itch on her back. It started as a mild distraction, a slight prickling tingle. The shirt she'd worn hadn't helped; it was some old Blondie concert tee she'd had since college that was whispery thin against her skin.

By the time the queue had moved from the heat of the outdoors to the air-conditioned indoor area that signaled to guests that they were edging closer to the ride with its brightly colored set-pieces and talking animatronic characters, Beth's back felt as if it were crawling with insects. She gave her back a quick scrape, rubbing up and down against a wooden post, but Marc urged her to keep up with the line. He then grabbed her by the arm and pulled her in close, his whisper hard in her ear. "Need to keep up. Seriously, what's wrong with you?"

"My back itches like crazy."

"Well, don't slow down the line like that. The girls are getting on up there. Just keep in front of me. I'll scratch it for you."

For any other couple, it would've been an adorable sight, the guy helping to ease away an itch on his wife's back. On the outside looking in, Beth thought she and Marc probably appeared playful and easy. But Marc's fingertips were hard and rough; they rapidly raked across Beth's sunburnt skin. She winced and withdrew from his painful touch. He reached for her again, but this time she dodged his hand and scuttled ahead, farther up the line.

"C'mon, Beth. Get back here. Let me just—"

"Nope, you're being rough. Not a good look for you."

Sadie turned and had her sister stop beside her long enough to give her parents an eye roll. "Oh, my God, would you guys hurry up! We're almost up front!" She gave Sylvie one of their shared, exasperated looks the two of them had often expressed in sync. "Told you we should've left them. They're so slow because they forgot their walkers." Sadie giggled and said something in her sister's ear, causing Sylvie to shriek and then promptly clap a palm over her mouth.

"You got lice, Mom? Issat why you're itchy?" Sadie said in a sing-songy voice.

"Or maybe it's scabies," Sylvie piped in, causing the two of them to then burst into a giggling fit.

"You need to stop that right now. That is *not* funny," said Beth as she maneuvered the girls around, having them walk along with her as Marc trailed right behind them, a dark look on his face.

She hated the balancing act, the ongoing effort to make sure the girls were parented as well as contemporary parenting could possibly allow—wiggle room and all—and the strain of making sure she didn't upset her husband.

Her husband and those dark moods that sprung up more often lately.

Those unpredictable moods.

"Happiest place on earth my fucking ass," he muttered, giving Beth what she hoped appeared to others as a playful shove.

In actuality, it was a push and it set her back on fire.

Saturday, ITINERARY: Waterpark, a.m. Rest at noon (no electronics, have twins read instead). Late lunch at Studios park. No more than 3 rides (Any argument & we cancel Sun. Princess Breakfast). Light dinner at hotel. Early bedtime.

Locked in the hotel room bathroom, Beth spent a good part of the late morning examining her back while Marc and the girls were at the waterpark. She had never seen a burn quite like it. Only a couple of days in, and the skin was already shedding in thin sheets. The skin beneath it had a light golden sheen and felt strangely silky, like it had been coated in a fine film of balm.

When Beth stepped under the shower's lukewarm water, it felt as if she'd just had acid poured down her back. She yelped and reached for the tap, quickly shutting the water off. She then stood there in the tub, panting. With her hands planted against the shower wall, Beth cooled her scorched back in the damp air.

"Beth!" Marc called from behind the bathroom door, rapping it loudly, "We're back, and the girls want to eat!"

Beth pushed away from the wall and quickly wiped at the corners of her teary eyes. If he saw her crying, he'd scold her for her "wayward decisions" in stupidly attempting to cool the burn down. She didn't want to hear it, that nagging tone he always used on her . . . his employees . . . his siblings . . . his continually ill mother . . . or anyone else he thought an idiot.

The problem with Marc was that, to him, basically *everyone* was an idiot. That is, except the girls of course. Those two could set fire to the world, and Marc would find a way to twist the details to make it seem as if society was solely to blame for putting the lighters in their hands.

That's just how it was with Marc.

"Beth?" The doorknob rattled. "What are you doing in there? Why's the door locked?"

"I need some privacy for shit's sake," Beth muttered as she stepped out of the tub onto the mat. She gently blotted herself down with a towel, taking care not to skim it across her back.

"Whassat?"

"Nothing. I just needed to go is all," she said in the door's direction.

It wouldn't matter. Marc hated locked doors, the front door being the sole exception. "We're married, and married people don't need 'privacy' between each other," he'd say. "And a locked door means there's no trust, just shame between us, and we shouldn't *ever* be ashamed of each other, Beth." It didn't help, of course, that his mother had had an affair with the neighbor's husband or that his father had kept a cache of his construction business's "investments" in a locked box in a hidden panel in the guest room bookshelf. It didn't help that every other person in Marc's entire family had an afternoon soap opera's worth of secrets that were never really secrets.

So, naturally, Marc had trust issues he refused to acknowledge and locked doors didn't help matters. Beth just wished that hadn't extended so bizarrely to bathroom doors, though she supposed that could've had something to do with her sister-in-law's habit of hoarding prescription painkillers, the habit that had killed her in the end.

His family issues had so quickly become Beth's issues.

Beth gave her shaggy mane a brisk rub with the towel and then examined her back once again in the mirror. The jagged, wispy sheets of the loose epidermis had shrunk in the water and had pilled. There were tiny, sticky gray balls dotted here and there around the patchwork of golden skin that had apparently been hiding there, dormant for—well, Beth didn't know for how long exactly. When she reached behind to touch a particularly noticeable bare spot near her shoulder, she was suddenly hit with a pulsing, tingling, pulling sensation in her groin. It was a shuddering climax that came with no preamble.

An orgasm just from touching her own skin.

It had been powerful enough in its quaking aftershocks that Beth wavered there for a moment and then had to sit on the toilet just to cool off, panting as she did.

There was another rap at the door, a soft one this time, coupled with a "Beth? Seriously, you okay in there?"

She could hear the girls whispering behind the door to their father. He shushed them and Beth heard him say softly, "She'll be out. She just needs a minute."

One of the girls giggled, a shrill, bubbling pop of sound. Sylvie. It was her trademark laugh, one of the few traits that set her apart from her sister. "Is she on her period?"

"Sylvie, that's disgusting. Don't say that," Marc scolded. "We don't talk about that at home, so we don't talk about it here."

"Why not? She might be on her period, Dad. Women need privacy when their vaginas are all bloody."

"That's enough!"

Sadie piped in, naturally defending her sister. "But what did Sylvie say that was wrong?"

"You know perfectly well what."

"No, we don't. Why don't you explain it to us, Dad?" Sadie said, her egging causing Sylvie to let out a stream of giggles.

Marc obviously wasn't interested in continuing the conversation, diverting his attention once again in his wife's direction. "BETH! For fuck's sake . . ."

Beth smiled at that. She liked it when he was uncomfortable.

She'd stay in the bathroom a little longer, exploring the newest intricacies of her own skin.

"Happiest place on earth," she said quietly as she touched herself.

Sunday, ITINERARY: 9am Princess Breakfast. Pack. Flight 3248 at 2:35pm (leave here at 11:45am sharp).

It was Sylvie who kept chewing with her mouth open.

Normally, Sadie was the one who'd wolf down her food, practically shoveling it all in, packing as much as she could in one, hefty bite. She often turned it into a contest with her sister, who would pretend to be aloof and uninterested, before she gave in. This time, however, Sylvie had the spark of mischief in her eye. Instead of challenging Sadie, Sylvie turned all of her attention on Beth as she scooped in bite after bite, scarfing down the familiar mouse head-shaped waffles. Beth stared at her when Sylvie grinned around a particularly gluey lump in her mouth.

"Mom, what's with your skin?" Sadie asked with a sneer. Now *that* was in character, at least, Beth supposed. Sadie was more inclined to go big when embarrassing Beth in public.

Beth stole a glance over at Marc

Marc, however, was too distracted to notice. He was catching up on the morning's headlines on his phone as he sipped from his coffee. Every so often, his eyes would flick in the direction of one of the Princesses who cooed and beamed, posing for a selfie with one of the other families there in the dining hall.

"It looks like . . . what's it called . . . when your skin's all different shades . . . like 'melatonin' or something."

"Melatonin's what you take for sleep, like a natural version of Ambien," Sylvie said in between bites. "That stuff that Mom takes. Right, Mom?"

"You mean vitiligo, sweetheart," corrected Marc, his focus still partially on his phone, but as ever, he wouldn't let his scrolling distract him from one of his favorite pastimes, correcting people.

"You don't need Ambien, Mom," said Sylvie, her eyes glinting with that spark that often got her in trouble. "You should just drink scotch like Daddy. You won't need a prescription for it."

Ten years old and she already knows what a sleeping pill is, Beth thought. *Ten years old and going through my bathroom medicine cabinet. How sweet it all is, and he doesn't give a shit about that.*

"Your mom just got too much sun," said Marc, finally setting his phone down to direct his attention on his wife, if only to chide. He

71

smirked at her. "I think she needs to remember to reapply the SPF every hour like it says on the goddamned bottle. But you know your mom, girls. Always in her own head and stubborn as ever."

Beth glowered at her husband. "*Again*, could you not use that language while out in public? You're setting a bad example."

Sylvie scoffed around another bite of waffle. "Yeah, Dad, could you not?"

Her sister chortled into her glass of orange juice.

"Well, you could've covered that up, Beth. That tank top isn't flattering on you. I mean, look at your skin, it's peeling all around your shoulders there. You should've worn something with sleeves like I told you."

Beth plonked her fork down on her plate, the shrill ring of it reverberating throughout the dining hall. The sound caused the girls to jerk in their seats, their eyes wide in a mixture of shock and anticipation. They both snuck a glance in their father's direction to gauge his reaction.

Marc's smirk had since formed into a tight line, teeth clenched, his stare hard.

In one swift motion, Beth was up out of her chair, quickly wiping her mouth with her napkin. She tossed the napkin, picked up her purse, and left her family to stew at the table without her.

"And that, girls," said Marc. "That is what ladies *don't* do when out in public. They don't make a scene. Speaking of scenes, Sylvie, for fuck's sake, chew your food with your mouth closed. You look like a cow chewing cud. It's disgusting."

Sadie snickered at her sister, who shot her dad a sulky scowl before focusing on her food again.

Beth was tempted to touch it. There, in the public facilities. Just the thought of it got her excited. She wouldn't be outright masturbating if she did it, or so she told herself. She'd locked herself in a stall, so it wasn't as if anyone would know what she was doing anyway, there, alone, away from her family.

Her family who simply couldn't stand her.

"You should do it," said a silky voice from beyond the stall door.

Beth spun around at the sound of it. "What?"

"Come out of there, Beth," the woman said.

"How do you—?"

The woman laughed. It sounded like tinkling chimes, strangely high-pitched and sweet. A Princess laugh.

"You should peel, Beth. Peel it all away."

Beth slowly slid the bolt aside and opened the door. Right outside the door, one of the Princesses stood there, facing Beth directly. A dazzling smile was planted on the Princess's face, stretching wide and showing off immaculate white teeth. The pastel blue dress she wore was fluffy with layers of crinoline and brocaded satin. Her platinum locks with heavy, thick bangs, had been set in a carefully curled updo with a wide blue headband as decoration. Yet what was most noticeable about the Princess was her radiant skin. It glistened in the low light of the ladies' room.

And her smell. She smelled of embers and spun sugar. Something wrong, something like home.

Beth couldn't help herself. She let herself be drawn in, and she moved right into the arms of the Princess, who held her tightly and stroked her hair while murmuring sweet, magical words.

"You're in the happiest place on earth, Beth," she said, nuzzling Beth's hair. "Everyone thinks it's all about the kids, but it's not." She pulled Beth from her to tenderly gaze at her, as if she had created Beth.

As if she had birthed her.

"It's about you. *You* need to be happy."

"I . . . I have a family," Beth whispered. "I should get back to them. They're waiting."

But the Princess had already begun peeling Beth's skin, her gloved hands working at her, unraveling her. It felt as if she was being scratched wide open with razor blades, like the Princess's talons were coming through the satin of the dress gloves. She didn't see any fingernails poking through the material, but she certainly *felt* them shedding her of her waste, shredding her entirely. The tangle of her skin, her cover.

It felt so good.

Everything was coming apart; everything was new again. Beth's body felt electric and a pulsing tingle consumed her. She didn't need the old skin anymore.

Happiest place on earth.

And the next layer was torn away and the one after that. And when Beth really began to bleed, off went the tendons, the nerves, and the tender meat.

When the Princess went for her heart, it was then when Beth

finally let herself go.

The man's eyes crawled all over the cleavage of the dark-haired Princess with the bare midriff and harem pants as she hugged his girls to her, a lithe arm around each of them, the three of them beaming at his camera phone.

Her thumbs idly stroked the back of the girls' necks, and she said with a tinkling laugh, "Say 'Princesses forever'!"

The twins' eyes had grown glassy when their father snapped the picture.

When the Princess broke away from the girls, she gave them a little wave, one last smile before she sauntered off to another table where a group of tiny tots squealed when they saw her coming.

The man checked the time on his phone and let out a low whistle. "You girls ready to go?"

The twins snapped awake and alert, as if they'd just come to life. "Yes, Daddy," they said in unison as they gathered their backpacks, and the man set down a tip, but not before lamenting aloud about the "goddamn price of a breakfast with no omelet bar."

For a brief moment, he could've sworn he'd forgotten *something*.

But that thought quickly diminished. After all, he supposed the resort would contact him if he'd left behind something valuable.

Whatever it was, it couldn't have been that important anyway.

THE DIFFERENCE BETWEEN CROCODILES AND ALLIGATORS

Malcolm Mills

"HONESTLY, I DON'T KNOW THE difference between a crocodile and an alligator." It's Matt's pick-up line, and it's somehow both genius and stupid. At the 2020 GatorCon, you must know the difference. Sure, some of us attend for the drugs, costumes, and orgies—indeed, many of us—but above all, we love crocodilians. Thus the genius of Matt's line is that it invites outrage, education, or laughter. Currently laughter. Tourists point and chuckle at the forty adults dressed as reptilians. Children film us with phones, as if we are more interesting than the national swampland around us.

I'm Terry and I'm on team croc. Crocodiles are better than alligators, if such superlatives matter (they do not) to anyone outside our convention. Crocs are generally larger and deadlier; their physical difference is an arrow-head snout with mud-gray scales, adept for the banks of the Nile or the estuaries of Australia. Alligators are chubby. Their snouts are wide and round. Though generally docile, they are prone to unexpected rage, sometimes at golf courses and hotel pools.

A woman in front of me swats the back of her neck; there is no insect, just moisture, her hair matted like tentacles. I think I recognize her, the flailing of her arms, her faceless and twisted neck, but no. She is not one of us; she is dressed in civilian clothes with no hint of reptile.

Matt is on team gator and dressed as such. The only odd element is that his suit comes with its own limbs; his arms and legs extend from holes, while cloth gator-nubs dangle beneath, rendering Matt more like a tailed spider.

We are all sweating, even as the Florida sun sets against the mangroves. I am surprised we still possess sweat. After the events of the steam room and the mad copulation of last night, I wonder how we recovered. Where did this extra sweat come from? It's been hard not to think of that steam room, especially since it's hard to piece together what happened.

Matt surveys our group, the long line. "Glen's not with us."

"No?" I look around. Glen was most excited about this tour of the Everglades. "Maybe that's him?"

At the end of our line, someone stands in a black gator mask, dark hoodie and sweatpants; surely the heat warrants removing the mask, but the figure is motionless, standing apart from the others. No one seems to notice him (her?); the others are slack-jawed, fanning themselves, grumbling how we should reschedule the convention for October (yes, and good luck finding reptile attractions open and affordable at that time, thank you very much).

"That's not Glen," Matt says. "Glen's always the red gharial." Ah yes, Glen and his underdog species—the gharial, a creature with a surreally thin snout found in Asia.

"Right." I remember last night. "Perhaps he's still with . . . you know." I look at Matt and wonder if he saw what I did.

"Hm?" We're moving up in the line. Tourists seem uneasy about boarding with us. They're letting us have our own boat. The lagoon shimmers.

"You know," I continue. "That saltwater mask. That cape of scales?" Matt had to have noticed the stranger in the spa.

"Oh. Hm."

"They were talking a lot," I try to say with no hint of jealousy. But I blush, recalling the cape's fall to the floor, the steam and bare skin, and the mask of the saltwater giant so vivid it had to have been taxidermy. My heart flutters, hoping the stranger will return and that I will be chosen tonight. I still have the key to the underground spa, and I don't think the hotel can change the lock so soon.

Finally we board the vessel, clanking across the metal platform with excited giggles. The on-board guide looks terrified, rubbing their National Park lanyard like a talisman. Our costumes make it hard to sit, and our bodies are worn from a week of intoxicants. We stumble, hooting and hushing. I risk looking back to the docks, to the land of normal people. The tourists gape and type on phones to research us. Their collars and buttons remind me of the costume I must don again soon—the return to a life that increasingly seems not worth living.

"At least I'm almost finished designing my Sim-Reptile for PC and PS4. The new graphics and prey AI really impressed the beta testers at PAX East."

"Huh?" Matt stares at me. "What?"

I freeze, for I have replied to silence, to nothing that has been said aloud. But everyone's too stoned to find it strange.

The steam rooms are a maze, and it is why the hotel was chosen. You've heard someone has rigged lights and gels; each room will have its own color. You enter from the basement of the Orchid Vale Resort, follow the signs for the spa, and pursue the figures dressed in green. Recreation-room hours be damned, for we have stolen the keys. Management has been compromised.

Doors designate 'men' or 'women,' but these are ignored; there is no discrimination, and the procession cannot be stopped. The threshold is upon you; you feel the steam, the moaning pulses that may be experimental techno or ambient reverberation from guests. You have been assured the rooms are vast, a labyrinth from which you must leave a trail to escape. You enter.

It's tempting to glide to the first attractive element: a nice shape, a certain mask, a beckoning gesture. Yet you should tour first, see it all. The blue room gives way to red. Steam is like fog here. You wonder, shall you remove more of your costume? Gloves and footwear litter the floor; here, a cartoon mask, the fabric tails of dragons. You see the first tangle of limbs, an amount that seems impossible to count, gyrating and sighing.

A cavern opens to a pool. Bright minds have engineered new ways to copulate while floating in water. Last year, it was a must-do—a dangerous delicacy, to mount one from behind with their head in the water like the creatures of the wild. It's an act of trust. You see two guests in the shallows performing it while three others watch. One appears to be drowning, but it's just the way they want it, their face hidden under a web of floating hair.

I'm snatched from my memory-fantasy, my pelvis still sore, humid on this bench of the boat. We remain docked in the shallows. Matt is flirting via vapid chatter. "Three? You think we'll see three gators?" "Perhaps we'll see a panther!" "Oh I'd like to see a manatee!" They're stupid, and we will only see birds and gators. Maybe a turtle. Others gaze about rapidly, pointing at lilies and logs, the same ones we've stared at for fifteen minutes.

Our guide is gone. Indeed there is no captain, no Everglades employee on the boat. Nothing to keep us from stealing it. I look at the dock, the reeds of the shore. I fear the park may banish us or call us drunk (we are). Or, they'll wait us out. The sun dips. Will they trick us and say it's too late, that the tours are over? Will we have time, as a back-up, to make it to Crocodile World off Longshore Avenue? It's a forty-minute drive. I'm furious.

But we're greeted by a new guide. Fresh-faced, her name-tag reads 'Elaine.' I'm taken aback, enthralled by her eyes, her mouth. I massage the back of my neck and try to look as cool as possible, as if my croc costume is worthy of respect. But Elaine's smile is unlaced with malice; she is warm, indeed appreciative, for we belong here. We want to see these swamps more than anyone. Ever.

"Hey guys! So happy to be your guide today on our little journey. My name's Elaine, and welcome to the Everglades National Park!"

The boat takes off and there's a cheer, followed by hushes, everyone's eyes on the water. Matt nudges me with his leg and cocks his head toward Elaine. I refuse the bait and pretend she doesn't appeal to me. If there is competition, I'd lose. His leg lingers against mine, our fabric touching.

I watch Elaine; she stares beyond us, at the docks of the park disappearing. We round a bend of foliage. I feel we are going faster than we should; the engine is startling wildlife. We steer back and forth, commanded by an amateur. I turn to see the driver, hidden behind a platform. I recognize parts of his dark outfit. It reminds me of the lone figure in black with the alligator mask. The boat slows and I'm relieved. Land and floating vegetation can barely be told apart.

"Hey guys," Elaine says. "So, I uh . . . I wanted to be sure that I had you for this . . . particular tour." Elaine dons a crocodile hat, gloves, and tail, procured like a magician. The audience gasps then cheers. One of us.

"Oh my god," Matt laughs. "Oh my god! This is gonna be fucking crazy."

But I'm staring at Elaine's figure. Everything fits; it must be her. I never saw her face, not until now, but it must be her.

"Matt," I say, "do you think she . . . have you seen her at the hotel? Is she a local?"

"Huh?"

"She's the one! From last night!" I'm hissing, barely audible, for secrecy may favor me.

"Dude, I do not know what you're talking about—"

"The woman with the scales, the cape. The saltwater mask."

"From last night?"

Not only does her skin tone match, it's her shape. Few of us are in what the evil world would call "good shape." Our costumes disguise this, but the stranger's costume displayed all. It was a body I'd never seen among us.

"That was a guy," Matt says.

"What?"

I'm annoyed. I'm missing what Elaine's saying; gator-gals are joking with her; the boat's drifting, engine off. Others crack open beers. Some spot floating alligators. I'm missing all of it.

"You're talking about the cape?" Matt squints. "That . . . that head like a—"

"Yes."

"That was a guy, man."

Drugs have affected all of us, but he's wrong.

"Too bad Glen isn't here," Matt says; his vacant eyes cruise the passengers. "He'd be able to say for sure."

I look at Elaine; her back is to me. Her hair sticks to her bare neck. Her shoulders do not move. She turns, looks right at me. It is her.

You're uncertain if you should remove more clothing. The drugs haven't kicked in yet; you're self-conscious. There's something you've stared at often in the mirror that you don't want others to see. In the dark, under fabric, it may stay that way. But as you pass through the rooms, you see others do not judge such corporeal aspects; all is open, all is loved.

The end of the maze is a dark room. Others have warned you; the farthest room is for those with the farthest limits. The room is pitch black. You wish to see, but have been told you cannot bring light inside. You step closer.

Before you enter, a stranger steps out with the head of a *Crocodylus australis*. The beauty freezes everyone in the room. What most wear is Halloween mishmash, the overstock outfit of Captain Hook's devourer. Your red gharial suit was 3-D printed by a cosplay company, but what the stranger wears is unreal; it is art. Scales so vivid they are taboo. They must be real, the real corpse of a saltwater crocodile, filleted and made a cape. The head is alive with dead black eyes, teeth emerging from its closed, angular mouth. There is no trace of a human until fingers emerge from the cape to dislodge it from a collar below the mask. The cape of scales falls to the floor to reveal a naked human body. Perfect.

The person's face is obscured under the crocodile's; the head turns, surveys the others. Acolytes in lust await direction. The arm of the stranger rises and drifts through the masses to point to you. The finger curls, beckons. The black eyes stare into yours. The figure steps back into the shadow of the final room. Everyone wants to follow, but none do. Only you.

It must be because of Glen's red costume. There's just nothing else to distinguish him. Dressing as a gharial is different, but Glen's face is so, so plain. Not even memorably ugly. And yet . . . and yet. Glen went into the room. He went into that fucking room.

I try to analyze whether I am plain (or very interesting?); the calculus of my chances computes, but I am missing the boat tour. The very tour that Glen organized. A coincidence? Glen, Glen, Glen. A surge of strangeness. What if Glen is on this boat? He needn't only wear red; he could be one of those masked. Is this some sort of trick? Or is he on another boat? Perhaps one already in the swamp. If indeed our guide Elaine is the stranger, then . . .

But what the hell would be the point?

Our boat turns too fast. This vessel cannot be meant for such speeds. No one seems to care; they're drinking. I look back at the driver, still hidden behind a platform. The roar of waves must be scaring animals, scaring everything, and defeating our purpose. Our guide's microphone is too loud.

"Amicia deLune was always fond of swimming, and she was fond of swimming here. In 1951, she wrote a generous check to the state of Florida, giving the state a vast stretch of land, this very stretch of land which we now travel upon."

Another fast turn around weeping trees; the wake of the boat stirs the willows. Night draws close, and what might be the price if we do not return on time? I lean close to Matt. "Don't you think we're . . . ?" But I see there's a hand under the fabric of Matt's pelvis, a caress from the neighbor to his left. Across the benches, limbs twist. Couples kiss.

Our guide continues. "By 1959, it was the goal of Ms. deLune to bring native species driven out of these lands back to their home. Unfortunately, with the suspicious and even ambiguous accident of her death—and I do say ambiguous for there is plenty of evidence of murder—she would not live to see the crocodiles return to Florida."

What?

"Excuse me," I say. "Could you repeat that? What are you talking about?"

She smiles, patient as a doctor. "Is there a problem?"

"Yeah, I think you're—well none of that is true, I'm afraid. I don't want to do your job. Maybe this is all a joke, but . . . "

"It's not a joke."

"I know my Everglades. There are no crocodiles."

She cocks her head. "Yes, there are."

"These wetlands have been strictly monitored for eighty years and no one just brings massive non-native species, well, maybe illegally . . . "

"They are native."

"Crocodiles are not native to America, no, I'm sorry."

Elaine laughs. Others laugh, too, even an odd laugh behind me that is inhumanly high-pitched.

"Of course they're native," Elaine says. "It just depends how far back you want to go."

We're having to talk loudly over the engine, and I hate how I sound when I talk loudly.

"How far—oh. You mean dinosaurs."

Others laugh, no longer disguising the fact they're fucking without contraception. I see the dark void of Elaine's eyes. Is this what she was talking about with Glen last night?

You can't see well in the final room, but there's a faint glow from outside. You can see the stranger's body in silhouette, the ridged head, the naked chest that hardly sweats, the legs postured like a mannequin.

"What is your name?"

The voice purrs. Of course the crocodile's mouth does not move; it's a mask, immobile. But the sound is not muffled; it echoes. There's a cool stone behind you, dripping.

"Glen," you say. "Hi."

The crocodile face stares back. You are not sure what part of their body to stare at.

"Hello, Glen," it says.

You have never initiated contact (last year this was not a problem), but the stranger makes no move. Their hands stay crossed behind their back.

"What's your name?" you ask.

The crocodile slowly shakes its head.

"No?" is all you can think to fill the silence. The light from outside dims; it's the others, peeking in, but the shapes don't match. There's a whisper reverberating behind you.

You feel it and say, "You can't tell me your real name?"

There's a breeze.

You go on, "Glen's not really *my* real name." The figure somehow grows more still. You have lost your advantage. "I mean," you try, "my real name's hard to pronounce. So I don't say it."

The stranger relaxes. "It is the same with me." But maybe it doesn't say that, maybe you just thought it. One of the stranger's hands moves to its thigh and you realize the stranger is now mirroring your position. The hand looks bloody, but it must be perspiration.

"Do you come here often?"

The stranger does not answer. You realize it is foolish to assume you were chosen just to talk. That is not what is done here. But what is? You gulp, shift, and casually widen your legs. The fabric of your red costume sticks to your flesh. You see the stranger also widen their legs, but the contents are in shadow.

"Will you tell me your real name?" The stranger has spoken.

Surely that's not all it wants, but you feel a gravity to the request. "What will you give me for it?" you say.

The stranger still has one hand behind its back. "What would you like?"

You study the stranger's body. With ease, you relay everything you'd like to do. The body laughs. "That is easy." Its other hand grabs your fabric and pushes, rips to expose skin.

Elaine's face has changed with the approach of night. She looks like someone I've seen before, like . . .

"I don't think Mr. Calls-me-a-Liar likes my tour."

Things have taken a terrible turn.

"I'm just saying," I backpedal to the region of an apology, "it's very cool, it's great. But we could enjoy this perfectly, without the—you know . . ." I try to look to the others for approval, but they stare blankly. "I mean, you didn't have to say *anything*, really. We'd be happy just to stare at the wildlife." Somehow my gator-friends have forgotten that I've organized this entire week. I have put in the painstaking hours of locating hotels, bribing officials, disguising debauchery, and hiring campaigns to sway public opinion. The accidents, the non-disclosures, the lies. I have spent my life for this, and they mock me.

In an accent that is British—though none of us are British—"He ought to walk the plank!"

I flail about to see who has spoken. I look to Matt; he bursts out laughing. It wasn't him, the voice was too high-pitched and deranged. "Walk the plank! Walk the plank!" Many are cheering. The boat slows and the crowd stands. Matt is cackling, spasming in pain with a smile that is too large.

"You, sir, do not belong here," Elaine says, but that is not her name. Everything about her is false. She points to the muddy banks. I can hear the insects. "You belong out there."

I'm being pushed; everyone has their masks on now.

"Come on, what the fuck. Stop it!" I protest, pushing back, rather too hard against one of them, and the individual smacks their head against a metal pole. Gasps resound with genuine alarm, like I am the one who's gone too far. I direct myself at the demon who's hijacked the tour.

"And you, what are you fucking doing here? What the fuck did you do with Glen last night?"

There's a silence as the others help the one I've pushed. The injured lies there, unmoving, definitely faking it. Someone removes the lizard mask, smacks the fat cheeks, but the face is blank, eyes open at the sky.

I repeat myself, louder, for this will clear up everything. "What the fuck did you do with Glen?"

Elaine or whatever-her-name-is looks at me with such convincing dismay that my theory crumbles. Her confusion confirms she may never have been in the spa last night. Or . . . or. She is very clever, indeed.

"You were! You were at the spa last night and—"

"What?"

Or perhaps they never exchanged names and that's why she's

staring like that. There's more gasping because the fallen one (Pam? Doug?) is bleeding and still not moving.

My back is pushed abruptly; a hand holds down my neck. I hear Matt laughing again, his voice rising to the impossible scream of a soprano. I stumble to the side of the ship; my legs are pulled, and I'm thrown over.

You are not where you were.

Perhaps you are deeper into the final room, the final cave. There is no light, but you can see. There is phosphorescent fungi, invisible to the human eye, but the stranger has shared with you the ability to see it. You will need it. You have been gripped by great strength and now it is your turn. You grip jagged rock and a delicate stream licks your fingers.

You must decide whether you are alone, and whether minutes or hours have passed. Something has happened with the stranger. You obeyed or protested. Either way, your clothes are gone. The costume has been shredded, and you feel its effects on your skin (as you wished). Your body is wet (also wished) and sore (wished). Try to remember what happened. Try, for it may be of grave importance. There is a deep sound of something large farther down the cave. You remember now, how it brought you here.

Though you can barely move, you have plenty of time to reflect. Is it all that bad? The rock is warm, and you are not alone. If what you wanted was indeed to copulate, to further your seed and spread your life, to feel pleasure and belonging, then . . . great. You have succeeded.

I am not drowned, for something saves me and pulls me to shore. I try to see what it is, but there's nothing—a tangle of algae, branches. My torn costume. The weight should have sunk me; it is not safe to be in costume and water (as we learned last year) and in a panic I've blocked from memory, I'm without costume.

I'm so shocked to be alive that I'm suspicious about whether I am. There's one light aside from the moon, a red glow in the distance. A wailing among the champion insects. I'm guided by voices (screams) and I swim to the red glow. How easy it is to swim! I feel I am bleeding, but it's like a jet propelling me. My spine twists. I glide, face in water, barely needing to breathe.

Their boat has crashed. There's a fire among mangroves and oil in the water. There's screaming from survivors, an unreasonable amount. On the shore, someone stands unnaturally tall, silhouetted against the flames; the figure carries heads by their hair—four in a fist. It places them on the altars of felled trees. A harmony of insects bends the melody. What emerges from the black water is white as marrow, and the heads are offered.

I am lucky, for a random direction takes me inland; a dirt road becomes jagged, unkempt concrete. I have found new attire, clothes that are quite perfect. It is not until I reach the glow of a lonely diner that I see my clothes are red. I pause, but the color is uniform, not stained, just an odd fashion choice made by a certain someone, someone who unwittingly lent them to me. I will buy new clothes, for the red draws too much attention. I feel my pockets: several wallets, plenty of cash.

Street-lamps disappear as dots down the road; beside me is a sign: BUS STOP, a vandalized bench where no one waits. The diner across the street smells delicious. Even after the events of tonight, I am starving.

I sit at the bar of the diner. The heat is nice. I am the only customer, and the only waitress speaks to me in Spanish. I reply in Spanish, struggling. She sees this, smiles, gives me a menu. Tendrils of dawn crawl over windows.

The diner could accommodate a hundred, but we are the only two here. The waitress smiles and watches me. I think she is waiting for my order, but even after I give it, she listens. Perhaps she noticed my limp and is worried; I am afraid to look at my reflection, to notice the blood I overlooked washing, blurred in the metal of a napkin canister. I turn the canister away, tidy my hair, smile.

"¿Estás bien?"

"Sí, sí."

"No emergencia? Accident?"

"No, no. Well, sí. Accidente, pero no mal. A boat. Agua."

She gasps, holds a hand over her heart. She speaks words of sympathy, and I reassure her gently not to call the police, no emergencia. Silence. Yet still she stares, waiting for something.

"It was an accident. I suppose. We were in the water."

An engine passes outside and I glance. It's the bus, but it doesn't stop. We are alone again. Coffee machines hum.

"We were having fun. You know. Romantic weekend. We'd been

looking forward to it. She wanted to."

I smile, and she looks at me with such kindness, a face that says: *You can tell me.*

I have never seen such kindness. Warmth and salt gather at my eyes. She waits and listens for more, even when there is only silence. "The back of her head was in the water for too long. No, I mean the front." (I see it when I blink; a web of hair that floats into what is a face, an expression.) "The front of her head. Her mouth. Her apparatus, to breathe—it all came undone in our movement.

"You'd laugh at the idea, but we were in love. We knew the risks. We were always the most alive in water. That's why, when there was a convention, we'd attend. She was an engineer and she engineered a device to float, to lie on her stomach. Why not her back so her mouth wouldn't be in the water? Well we'd done it like that. We'd tried everything, but we wanted to fuck just like they do, in the water."

I expect a reaction, but my listener's gaze is unmoved. At any moment, if anyone enters, I am ready to stop. I close my eyes, and I can see the back of the head quite clearly.

"We knew it was dangerous. But it was also her design. She only had to lift her head a bit, and she'd breathe." (I recall her trying) "But . . . well. I couldn't tell the difference. Pleasure and pain, how can it be read from the back of a head? To stop, to continue. What's the difference? Maybe there isn't one."

I look at my listener; her face is unreadable. An AC kicks on by itself.

"No," I say. "You're right. Of course there's a difference."

(There is no mistaking the panic of flailing arms, a spine pushing against—)

"I loved Elaine. And it was my interpretation of our love (stop talking) that thought . . . well . . . if anything was going wrong. We knew the risk. I thought she was fine. (you're filth) I couldn't tell. It felt perfect. At the time." (Afterwards, she drifts, looks fine)

I doubt my listener can understand me. But I feel much better. I needn't repeat myself . . . It's over.

But then I study her face, and I know the waitress has understood everything. She sees I see it. Her expression clarifies itself: sadness. Forgiveness. Genuine forgiveness. She forgives me.

I sip my coffee, nod. Thanks.

But perhaps she is not as stupid as she looks. Perhaps she thinks that expression will appease me. Hmmm.

THE DIFFERENCE BETWEEN CROCODILES AND ALLIGATORS

The difference between alligators and crocodiles is that alligators are content to eat fish. Crocodiles hunt what lives on land.

We are still alone in the diner. All is still, until she leans close to collect my menu.

THE CUCUY OF CANCUN
V. Castro

I LOUNGE ON A SUNBED covered by a towel with the words *Daytona Beach* splashed across in neon blue. But I have never been to Daytona Beach, nor do I have the faintest idea where it is. Two young people speaking English laugh and splash each other as a waiter, Lorenzo, brings out another bucket filled with Coronas buried in ice. He avoids eye contact because these assholes have a way of being rowdy and rude. Entertainment is as cheap as their manners. I'd only intervene if I caught a prick getting rough with the staff.

One of them, a skinny gringo with pimples on his lobster-colored back, attempts to rap to trap music that plays loudly from a small speaker attached to a phone. I smile because it's not even noon and I can smell their intoxication, sweat, and desire for sex. The only missing ingredient is their fear.

I want to nuzzle in their heart chambers and soak in their blood. I want to fill this grubby, over-chlorinated pool with their limbs. Their severed heads will float like abandoned inflatable toys. Some of them will have their flesh made into strips of jerky while I slurp on their chilled brain matter like a piña colada. In the morning, I will moisturize my tan skin with their melted down fat because it prevents me from burning beneath the hot Mexican sun.

I am the Cucuy of Cancun.

Do you know what a Cucuy is? It is a boogeyman, a harbinger of nightmares that skulks in the dark. I am not a man and I detest the dark, but I am a nightmare. Older than humans, I remember what you now call Mexico before Chichen Itza and Tenochtitlan existed. There were only the primordial creatures, the earth, and pure oceans after the mighty beasts died out and the frozen wasteland melted. There were no borders or passports. Then humans moved from their bellies to two legs, and in time spread like toxic ash across the land.

Like a true predator, I remain still and silent on my sunbed, watching behind heart-shaped sunglasses so dark no one can see my eyes.

By nightfall, one of them will be alone—too drunk to piss or stand—and that is when I slink next to them. My bikini top and frayed cut-off shorts distract them. My elongated fingers are topped with hooked nails strong enough to cut through jungle vines and used for slicing like a machete.

I hate spring breakers. Their waste, their noise, their entitlement. They remind me of the invaders who colonized this part of the world just when us dark creatures were beginning to get our groove on with the humans. All of us non-human creatures and shifters were driven from sight and from our homes. We call the margins home, scary stories you tell your friends. That is when we began to feed upon them. You encroach on our habitat and we will encroach on your liberty by taking your life.

Ages passed under occupation, war, disease, and democracy. With no control to stop it, the first resorts cropped up, which were new invaders of sorts. Sun-lotioned, money-waving gluttons wanting to be served during their vacation from their lives. My taste for flesh began as I saw other supernatural creatures in the dark partake with delight. How could I not? Revenge is best served raw.

Today my sights are set on this group of three. Very rarely do I fuck any of these young ones. I prefer the middle-aged married folk, sex-starved and desperate to have a break from their hectic rat-race lives. Second marriage bachelor and bachelorette parties are the best. Oh, and business conferences. Those, I fuck and consume. When they think they are catching feelings for me is when I catch their tongues between my teeth and pull. All a tragic accident. Hold my margarita on the rocks while I cry.

I promise beautiful views from the 18th hole on a perfectly mani-cured golf course only to lure them to the lagoons where the croco-diles dwell. I take what I want and leave the scraps for the animals—animals that are in a constant state of anxiety with golf balls plunking into their homes and the sound of mowers cutting grass non-stop. Poor beasts.

I continue to observe the three while listening to Depeche Mode's "World Through My Eyes" on an iPod from one of my victims. The synth beat makes my sweaty, sizzling body move in place and I tap my toes. I like the vocals of David Gahan; the deep, rich tone makes me think of a priest who worshipped me centuries ago. I tested his faith and the lengths he would go to for the pleasure of my hands and mouth. In the end, I had to put him out of his misery. He could not believe his God would allow a creature like me to exist.

By the expression on the female's face, I can tell the young woman is complaining about the food. The one with the pimpled back is now slathered with white sun lotion post sunburn and he pulls Lorenzo to the side to whisper in his ear. Lorenzo shakes his head and glances toward me before shuffling off with half-eaten plates of food. I know exactly what the spring breaker has asked. After another bucket of beers, they will slowly leave, and I can formulate my plan.

It is nearly 4 PM by the time they gather their belongings to make their way back to their rooms. One stays behind. He remains rather sedate, more interested in his phone and his beer. He wears a pastel pink polo shirt and simple board shorts. Lorenzo returns to clean their mess. The quiet one stops him. Lorenzo keeps shaking his head even when the polo-wearing guy flashes a wad of dollars. This is my moment.

I jump from my sunbed and readjust my bikini bottom before approaching the two men.

"Lorenzo, water, please?" He leaves with a look of relief to see me saving him from this uncomfortable situation.

"You know, just because we are south of the border doesn't mean drugs grow on trees."

The young man blushes. It is the same shade of pink as his shirt. "Why do you think . . ."

"Save it. I've lived here all my life. I'm not an idiot."

He looks like a kid being told off by an adult.

"May I ask what you are looking for? Snow or grass?"

His eyes widen before looking around to see if anyone is in ear shot.

"I don't know. It's not for me. Um. I guess both."

I motion him to follow me to my sunbed. I know he is watching my wide ass jiggle. From the pockets of my shorts, I pull out a tiny packet of cocaine and half a joint.

"This is all I have for now, but if you tell me where you will be tonight, I might have more."

He reaches for both. I put them back into the pockets of my shorts. "Later. Tell me where you will be."

"The plan was to go to some bar, Amigos, for a sunset party that starts at 6 PM, but after that I'm not sure. You wanna meet at the bar?"

"No. How about here, say midnight?"

He glances shyly at my breasts then tries to get a look at my eyes beneath my sunglasses and my Princeton baseball cap.

"Hey, Princeton. Did you go there?" He gives me a look like it is inconceivable that someone like me would be an Ivy League graduate. My face remains blank.

"I only ask because I go to Penn, in Philadelphia."

Philadelphia. I know of that place.

"Midnight. Room number?"

"Oh, right. 95."

I lie down on my sunbed and put on my earbuds. He should get the hint he can leave now because he is blocking my sun. All I need to do now is wait. It gets them every time, a little bag of flour and rolled paper filled with oregano. Dumbasses.

When the sun sets, I retreat to my room for a siesta until it is time to feed. Refreshed from my dreamless sleep, I change into a black string bikini top and matching black shorts that are cut high on the ass. They might as well be big underwear. But I like how I look in them, how they make me feel. I wear black because blood stains.

I bring a different iPod from another victim. Although, this one I did not kill. He was the only black kid in a group that acted like he didn't belong. I exchanged his life for his music because it spoke to me. He also had to promise to never speak about me; otherwise, I would hunt him down in the middle of the night. The sight of my nails stained with his classmate's blood was enough to keep him fearful of the dark for the rest of his days.

The motel is dark and quiet except for the ice machine and distant bass pumping from the clubs along the beach. Lorenzo waits for me by the pool. I hand him three hundred dollars before kissing him on the cheek. He walks away to keep the area around room 95 free from guests. His family owns this motel, my home of sorts.

I knock on the door. The young woman from the pool answers. "Guys, did you call for housekeeping?" She looks me up and down, "Or a hooker?"

Her blood will taste even better after this insult. A housekeeper? Do I look like a housekeeper? A hooker? Everything I own is taken from the discarded luggage from my victims. Women not from here. Her judgment is sand in my eye. Now she will pay for that.

"May I come in?"

"I guess." She opens the door wider and I step in. The skinny obnoxious one and my pink Penn student sit on the bed, scrolling through their phones.

"Hey. You showed up. Wasn't sure if it was real."

The young woman scowls before turning away to mix herself a drink of Stoli vodka and cranberry juice.

A small speaker is to my right, on the dresser with the TV. The rest of the place is a mess with towels and clothes tossed in cyclone fashion.

I take out my iPod. Jay Z's "I Just Wanna Love Ya" will do just fine for this occasion. I enjoy rap as much as I like Depeche Mode and Santana. I turn the volume all the way up, signaling to Lorenzo lounging next to the pool that it is about to begin. My breathing is growing rapid, as is my heart rate. The muscles in my throat relax.

The skinny one turns his cap backwards and begins to bob his head as he approaches me. His eyes scan my flesh on show; the bikini top contains even less than my shorts. I allow him to awkwardly try to dance with me, a grind that wouldn't even remotely feel good if we fucked. "You got the party bags, baby? I'm thinking you should stay and have some fun with us. Becky won't mind."

"No. That wasn't the plan, Brock."

I lick my glossy pink lips before smiling and removing my sunglasses. They are jade marbles with obsidian pupils in the center. There is no time for him to scream before the bottom and top rows of Mako-shark-like teeth rip out his vocal cords in one swift bite. Blood sprays across the room like candy from a broken piñata. My right hand plunges into his chest. I possess his heart and I shatter it with a single squeeze.

Becky screams then tosses the bottle of vodka at me. For these occasions I wear cowboy boots. In two long strides I'm close enough to Becky that I can pin her against the wall. All her breath escapes. She tries to recover, but I grab her by the neck. "Little bitch, I am not a hooker nor a housekeeper. I am a Cucuy that has forever been, and will forever be. Your existence means nothing."

"I'm sorry, I'm sorry!"

I hate when they beg. With a swipe of both of my hands, I break her neck then let her body fall to the floor. From my peripheral vision, I see the Penn student retreat to the bathroom. He is probably trying to get Wi-Fi or a signal. Too bad I have thought of everything. This is a dead place when it's feeding time.

I knock the door in with one kick. He is sitting on the toilet frantically trying to find help on his phone. He is on the verge of tears, seeing me for what I am. The jade in my eyes glows and reflects his fate. Jade is sacred, you know. Blood speckles my skin and clothes. But I know it is my full mouth and nails, dripping crimson, that frighten him the most. "Wait here."

I back out of the door so that he never leaves my sight. I drag the girl by her hair to the front of the bathroom threshold before straddling her. A single punch to her chest reveals her heart. With a second thrust, I remove her liver. Filled with lust, I consume both organs as they limply wobble in my hands. The flesh rips; small pieces flop between my breast and tumble to my thighs. Both morsels are gone within minutes.

"What is your name?"

He is shaking, looking at me instead of at Becky's body as he clutches his phone like a rosary.

"Thomas."

I lick my fingers and then point to the sink. "Do me a favor and hand me one of those."

With a hand that won't stop trembling, he hands me the glass. I snatch it from him and dip it into Becky's chest cavity, which is filled with pooling blood.

"Sit down. Next to me."

He obeys wordlessly, sniffly from his crying.

"Tell me about Philadelphia and your school."

"Um. It's a big city. Not as big as New York. Good restaurants. Really cold in winter."

"Cold? Oh no."

"Not all the time. Just in winter. My school is great. One of the best in the country. My parents went there. Why do you ask?"

"Have a drink."

He doesn't move. The expression on his face says he is scared shitless and confused by this conversation.

"I said have a drink with me."

He scrambles to his knees and grabs a bottle of tequila off the bed. It's Patron. Good.

"Here is the deal. I'll spare your life, for a price."

"Anything! Please. My family has a lot of money. Here. Want this watch? It's a Rolex I got for high school graduation."

"I don't want your fucking money. I want to see your world. Take me to your home."

Thomas looks confused again. "But you don't have a passport. You will get stopped, or even detained at the airport."

"You think anyone could stop me?" I raise my hand, dripping in blood, and show my jagged-toothed mouth.

He gulps a mouthful of tequila with eyes quivering. "I suppose not. We will have to drive maybe. What will you do when we cross the border? And why do you need me?"

"Sounds like Philadelphia is a fun place. A college town. There is somewhere in Philadelphia I have wanted to visit for a long time, but this will be my first time away from here, and I would like a guided tour. Once there, I will do what I have always done. Feed. Live."

I lift myself from the dead body to sit, cross-legged, in front of Thomas. He still doesn't move, but at least he is no longer trembling. I take the bottle from his hands, necking it for a good, long drink, and then hand it back to him with smears of blood on the top. "Your turn."

He stares at the blood he will have to taste. Small eddies of red float in the bottle. I can tell he is contemplating wiping it first. Without looking at me again, he drinks.

"Great. Tomorrow you will help Lorenzo and I clean this mess. Finish off your vacation with me. There is no way you could have known how or why your friends went missing if you spent the entire night in my bed. Multiple witnesses can attest to that."

He doesn't move. He is wondering if there is any way out.

"Grab your shit. Let's go." He moves quickly now; this is his only chance at surviving.

Before we walk out, I rummage through Becky's luggage, taking only her beach bag. I shut the door behind me and remove the numbers on the front. At the end of the week, when the new guests arrive, the configuration will be different. But I won't be here to enjoy the fresh arrivals.

I search the beach bag from dead Becky. She had decent taste. I slip on a spaghetti strapped sundress and floppy red hat that matches the new sunglasses named Prada. I twirl in front of the mirror, admiring the way the sun has brought out the red hues in my dark brown hair. Next stop is The Pink Agave Motel in Philadelphia, USA.

Even the Cucuy needs a vacation.

TAYLOR FAMILY VACATION '93
Jeremy Herbert

NOBODY ELSE IN THE FLAMINGO Court continental breakfast nook would've noticed twelve seconds missing from their Scotch-brand T-120 videocassette except "Double Digit" Daniel Taylor, CPA. Most consumer-grade camcorders rounded remaining footage to the minute, but Daniel knew the RCA CC 310 Pro Wonder better than most people knew their extended families. He started his research the day Amy told him she was pregnant. Whoever was on their way, Daniel wanted to meet them with nothing less than the highest audio-visual fidelity of 1988. The Pro Wonder was the only choice. 1/60 shutter speed with optional slow-motion. Power zoom, with an 11-to-88-millimeter focal length. One-inch monochrome viewfinder. It counted time in seconds as opposed to minutes, but for a man named "Double Digit" Dan by coworkers in semi-sincere awe, an extra calculation was just another feature. The only number that didn't add up was the price, but Dan told Amy he found it on sale. Besides the timestamp resetting when you weren't looking, the Pro Wonder was still a good camera.

A good camera with twelve seconds less tape in it than when "Double Digit" Dan turned it off last night.

The tasteful black and white monolith of the Pro Wonder took up most of Daniel's place at the table. He hadn't turned it back on since waking up and noticing the discrepancy. He also hadn't looked away

96

from it.

"Your eggs are assuming room temperature," said Amy, chin in hand. She was watching a pale tourist in high white shorts figure out the microwave across the room.

"I don't mind," said Daniel, shoveling a jaundiced hunk into his mouth. "They're better this way," he said, tasting nothing.

Amy gave him the look. He hadn't seen it in a while. Half accusation, half lament. *How could you say such a thing? How could I marry such a man?* Daniel smiled and let the eggs spill out of his mouth into a napkin. Amy missed it, already back to watching the microwave, but Josh giggled. The kid was an easy mark, dad his favorite comedian. Daniel glanced at him sideways—their agreed upon punchline for all slapstick—and the kid lost whatever decorum he had left. None of the other early-rising tourists even noticed. They had unruly audiences of their own to attend to.

Twelve seconds. He almost forgot about them. That's what vacation was all about, though, forgetting the things otherwise unforgettable. He had promised Amy he could forget. But not before watching those twelve seconds.

Daniel casually dialed down the speaker volume on the Pro Wonder. He rolled the tape back without looking, then tilted up the viewfinder. Nestled safely within the rubber eyepiece, a colorless Josh stomped around a hotel pool like he owned the place. Daniel rewound too far, but he didn't mind watching Josh wave, Daffy Duck floaties flapping on his little arms. Josh shouting *Donald Duck* in fuzzy silence. The Disney duck was his favorite, but the elder Taylors couldn't find those floaties anywhere. Daffy was good enough for Josh, who promptly turned and flung himself into the water. As the videographer lunged and the Standard-Play world blurred blue, Dan noticed the date was messed up again. He clicked his tongue a few times, the only way "Double Digit" Dan ever admitted frustration, and fast-forwarded. Amy pointing with Josh at the Epcot golf ball. Josh getting his brown mess of hair further messed by a bearded man with a dragon on his arm. Minnie Mouse as big as Godzilla speeding down Main Street USA. A pan across the endless sea of baseball caps and oblivious kids riding their parents' shoulders like gently bucking broncos, then a flurry of pastel t-shirts as the camera bounced away. All in Benny Hill double-time. Then squirmy black. 2:49 AM. 5/18/93. The correct time. About seven hours ago that morning.

Daniel leaned over the viewfinder like a microscope and watched the grainy little void. The Pro Wonder's auto-focus was second to none, at least in 1988, but black was black. A white orb streaked across the nothing, then inched back in from the side. Fighting the camera's weight. Steadying. A layer of fuzz peeled away from the orb, gave it focus. Sharpened it into a supernova above a hundred stars. A light pole over the hotel parking lot, scattering across a gray field of hoods and windshields. It was the view from inside the Taylor family's hotel room.

Daniel looked up at his wife and his son and tried to smile. Amy cocked an eyebrow at him over her orange juice. Josh was just happy to be involved. Daniel turned back down to the viewfinder and finished his lukewarm coffee.

A black edge cut off the bottom of the shot and sent the auto-focus reeling. Then the edge fell and the parking lot came together again. Whoever was holding the camera couldn't keep it steady over the sill. They couldn't have been more than three feet tall, give or take.

Daniel turned to Josh, who was ready for Dad's callback joke to the eggs. But Dad didn't waste any more food.

"Josh," said Daniel as calmly as he could.

"Not at breakfast," said Amy.

If he asked his son why he was playing with the camera, Amy would ask why their son was awake at three in the morning. Daniel would remind her how expensive the Pro Wonder was, minus the $200 he lied about, and she would accuse him of caring more about his camera than his boy. It wasn't worth it, not yet. Maybe he had trouble sleeping like his old man. Until the last year or so, Daniel dreamed about receipts that ran on forever with numbers he couldn't read. Maybe Josh wanted a turn as the family videographer. Maybe he'd inherit the mantle in a few years. Nothing wrong with that. Good for him.

Daniel managed a genuine smile this time, proud of his son. It was enough to turn Amy's attention back to her orange juice.

All the other parents in the breakfast nook, which was nothing more than a palm-accented corner of the lobby, yelled at their kids to eat their Corn Flakes and to keep their stuffed cartoon characters out of their respective mouths. But not Daniel and Josh Taylor. They were alright.

The rest of the day was 351 seconds long. A line of paintbrush palm trees shimmying in windy unison. Several zooms on a gift shop shaped like a wizard. A round of miniature golf at a place called Congo River, with a crashed plane smack on the front. Several zooms on the plane. A nearly identical shot at the beginning of every hole, with Amy lining up a putt and Daniel saying, "Let's see a hole-in-one." The first few holes, she smirked at the camera. Then she said, "Stop." Then she didn't look at the camera at all. On hole 15, she shook her head. On the last hole, she stuck out her tongue. Another gift shop, this one shaped like a giant orange. A wide shot, but not wide enough, cutting off the round peak. A wider shot to get it all in. Rows of souvenir alligator heads. A finger poked one of the teeth. Off-camera, Amy said, "Gross." One last sweep of the parking lot— another hotel, highway, more hotels, then crates of incandescent citrus outside the big orange—all ending on a mural of two kids picking fruit under a hand-painted slogan. *Take Some Home.*

Daniel wedged a chair under the doorknob that night. As he dragged it across the room and left fresh tracks in the matted carpet, he justified his paranoia. He spent fifty, sometimes sixty, hours a week staring at numbers and making sense. That's what kept him going; everything made sense if you carried the decimals right. Josh played with the camcorder. That made sense. A chair under an already chained and dead-bolted door, though, couldn't hurt. It was a hedged bet. Amy didn't ask.

She changed her clothes, washed her face, took her pill, and fell asleep in her bed before Daniel even turned on the TV. Josh was next in the rotation, struggling to pull his pumpkin head through a t-shirt with an off-model Scooby-Doo on it. The boy gave up halfway through the fight and embraced his new existence as a ghost with hair. He ran a few tight laps haunting the sink, then heaved himself up onto the bed he shared with Daniel and let out a dwindling, "Booooooo."

Daniel pulled his pajamas from the bottom drawer, navy shorts and a pink athletic shirt that was red once, then looked at the Pro Wonder sitting on the lopsided table by the window.

Taking the two-pound battery off its charger and sliding it back into the camcorder, Daniel rewound to the gator teeth. He mentally dubbed the silent *gross* and waited until the square screen went blank. End of recording. Daniel memorized every number until his right eye ached and then put the battery back where it belonged at this time of night.

Daniel put himself back where he belonged this time of night, too, under covers artfully polka-dotted with cigarette burns, pinned to the mattress by a tiny arm across his stomach, watching the tourist channel on mute.

He didn't know if it was actually called the tourist channel, but that's what he called it around his coworkers and all of them who'd made the pilgrimage knew exactly what he meant. It was wall-to-wall commercials. Go-karts on International Drive. Dinner theater with murder and all-you-can-drink beer. Entire buffets dedicated to cuisines Daniel couldn't place on a map. Josh loved it because something flashy, new, and aimed squarely at his four-year-old brain was only ever thirty seconds away. Daniel loved it because it felt like watching a transmission meant for extraterrestrials. It was soothing, somehow. The white noise of a world where even credit card bills seemed imaginary. Daniel fell asleep after an ad for a gift shop that sold only shells. He didn't dream at all.

Daniel got up early to check the camera, not that he slept much anyhow. Twenty-two seconds gone. He rewound a little too far again and almost missed the play button with his finger.

Gators. Teeth. *Gross.* As expected. Then another white orb burning a hole in black. This one was more unnatural. Not a star. A square. Flickering. Draining the last light out of the dark until a commercial formed between the tracking bars. A mean knife sliced a mean ribeye and a Chinese chef smiled uncomfortably.

Daniel looked up from the camera to the TV he left on last night. It was off now. Now playing in the viewfinder.

The videographer let the commercial finish, tried zooming in on the locations at the end. They were still too short to steady it. Daniel could just make out *I-Drive.* He glanced across the room at the four-year-old lump in his bed.

Daniel smiled—Josh was experimenting with his craft.

Another zoom back out as the next commercial silently started. Letters bounced on screen and shimmied between flickers: *What's a Wet n' Wild?* But before the ad could answer, the Pro Wonder panned away into the dark. Daniel squinted in tune with the auto-focus, scouring the room for the faintest pixel of life. A gray ridge faded out of the black. Something caught in the TV's nuclear glow. Writhing and wriggling. Then rolling over.

Amy swaddled in her comforter.

Daniel snorted a laugh and caught himself before he woke anybody up. He'd never seen his wife presented like a deep-sea discovery before. It suited her. She could never see it.

Then the shot tilted, no, *lifted* up. As high as the arms of a three-foot-tall videographer allowed. Farther still. Until whoever was holding the camera had to point it down at Amy.

The Pro Wonder turned away to the TV again. The water park commercial wasn't over. A lazy dad held his confused toddler by the arm as they floated aimlessly on matching innertubes. A grown man's hand reached in, blotted out the screen, and shut it off.

Daniel set the camera down quietly and let out three hushed clicks of frustration to keep from imploding. He looked at the door—still jammed with a chair and double-locked. Even if somebody could beat that, there was no way they could reset it on the way out. *A stranger was in this room.* He clicked the hollow thoughts away. Somebody was there. He even had proof. But he didn't need to let that eat him alive.

His eyes wandered across the beds. A crease of sunlight slipped past the curtain and cut Amy in half at the waist. Josh, lying sideways and face down, dodged it in his sleep.

The lonely quiet of a forty-dollar rack-rate motel settled in. Bedsprings aired belated grievances. A TV hummed white noise through the left wall. Locks clattered through the right.

The right wall, with the adjoining door to the next room over, which "Double Digit" Dan Taylor never thought to lock.

Dan flung himself over Amy's bed, caught his knee on the mattress, and tailspun to the carpet.

"Hey!" Amy jolted up.

Dan crawled, then flung himself at the door as fast as his socks allowed. With one momentous twist, he threw the deadbolt and waited.

Silence on the other side.

"What are you doing?"

He heard the distant cry of a turned doorknob in need of oil, but not the one in front of his face.

Dan looked at the other door, still lovingly barricaded.

A shadow blinked past the thin line of day between curtains.

Dan threw himself back to the carpet, crawling until he could run, stubbing his toe on Amy's bed.

"*Dan,*" said Amy upon impact.

Dan didn't hear her over the sound of his security chair bouncing off the drywall. By the time she said it louder, he was outside.

"Double Digit" Dan was alone on the second floor of the

Flamingo Court, alone on the south side at least. Across the way, a bronzed stick figure shook a breeze into a sagging tank top and waved. Dan didn't return the gesture.

The parking lot below was quiet, shushed by up-and-at-'em traffic on 192. Any cars destined for a decent spot at one of the parks were already gone. An elderly lady in head-to-toe mint held the lobby door open for a little girl. Dan didn't hear any running. No breaker or enterer.

Dan put his hand on the black metal railing and let it burn him calm. Not even nine and it was already, what, eighty out? It was going to be a hot one. On the way to Universal he'd stop at a 7-Eleven for sunscreen. Amy tanned, but Josh turned pink as ground beef in direct sunlight.

Keys jangled.

Dan flinched.

A red Chevy Lumina with Florida plates MKK 2982 three spots up, five over. The driver wiped the key on the edge of a white golf shirt with a little alligator on it. Satisfied, he tried the key again. But he didn't turn it.

The driver looked up at Dan. Toward him, at least. A plastic visor blacked out his face to the nose. The man with the alligator on his shirt smiled a white smile.

Daniel spun on his sock, tearing a hole clean through the heel, and grabbed the equally hot door handle. He shook it and shook it. No luck. No *key*.

"Amy, get the camera." Loud. As loud as "Double Digit" Dan ever got. Amy opened the door without the camera and got loud, too.

"What is wrong with you?"

Daniel couldn't give her the correct answer, no matter what was already in the Pro Wonder. The vacation would be ruined. The home video, too. The sensible Daniel Taylor couldn't have that. The only hard evidence was his eye-witness account of the alleged perpetrator's fashion sense. What good was that?

"The sunrise," said Dan. "I wanted to get it on tape."

"It's nine."

"I know," he said, knowing Josh had to be awake by now, listening to his parents talk loudly and only understanding the volume. "I overslept," he said, knowing that Amy at least listened to him. She might've even trusted what he told her about the weather and the Wall Street Journal, but she hadn't truly believed him in a long time.

"Ready to go?" he asked in his pajamas.

Dan put on his turn signal just shy of the 7-Eleven on 535 and Amy asked why. He said sunscreen. She said don't bother. He got back over and onto I-4, driving in silence until he found a distant spot in the Universal lot.

"Do you need to bring that," said Amy, no need for a question mark, as Daniel hefted the Pro Wonder on his shoulder. He answered with a wide shot, framing her like a fashion model against the endless cars and picket fence palm trees a mile off. The frame tightened on her face, all apparent emotion hidden behind mirrored aviators but more than implied by hard eyebrows and pinched nostrils. She turned away from her close-up. Dan stopped recording and clicked his tongue.

He hit the red button again to take in the Universal Studios arches. From speakers Dan couldn't see, Doris Day hipped slow Hooray for Hollywood. Maybe it was the tempo or the stone gargoyles holding up the highest arch, but through the viewfinder, Dan thought the entrance looked like the gates of an art-deco graveyard. He preferred the view from his parking space, when it was no more imposing than the Lincoln Log village Josh had built in the den a year ago and never cleaned up.

The next time Daniel pressed record, he was walking past a hat shop shaped like a hat. If he wasn't so focused on keeping the camera steady, he would've smiled.

Yogi Bear won the trust of a reluctant toddler by shaking his belly like a hula hoop. Dan wanted Josh to go in for a hug, but the kid didn't trust the big-headed folk yet.

Fifteen seconds on a pan across the park lagoon. A banana-yellow speedboat churned wake past whipping flags. The Ghostbusters hearse rolled toward Mel's Drive-In and squealed its siren at a sock hop in progress. Amy leaned on the railing of a New England boardwalk, the billow of her cotton shirt caught like a sail. Dan stopped recording, but kept watching, wondering when he last kissed her and noticed.

Four seconds recording a blow-up Beethoven, peeking over the roof of the animal show amphitheater like a benevolent god, drooling on the faithful with a cartoon tongue.

Eight seconds on Mr. Ed or a decent impersonation. There was a whole roster of animals doing goofy things; Dan didn't need to belabor the point on a horse that flapped its gums.

Twelve seconds on an orangutan that flapped its gums.

Josh could barely contain himself, that gatling gun chuckle. Dan kept waiting to see a head turn around in blurry close-up to glare at the noise, until he noticed a specific head down in front. Sweat-matted gray hair poking past a white polo collar. A plastic visor looped around the back of his scalp.

What color was his visor? Dan could recite the license plate like a phone number, but color? It was all black-and-white through the viewfinder.

Forty-four seconds of tape waiting for the guy to turn around.

"How do you think they train a dog to do that?" asked Amy.

The visor turned to the side a little, tipped down to a kid next to him. A dim profile at best.

Then he made digital eye-contact through the Pro Wonder. It was quick, instinctual, just as fast as he looked away. But it was enough. Dan tried to zoom out, but his fingers shook themselves off the controls. Without looking at his wife or his son, Dan lowered the camera, watched Lassie limp across the stage, and plotted.

"I need to use the bathroom," said Dan after two hours of following the man around the park, waiting for nature to call, and now seeing that visor bounce over the crowd toward a men's room done up like a Manhattan waterworks.

"Alright. Gimme the camera." Amy put her hands out as she squatted on the nearest bench.

"I got it."

"That thing's like fifty pounds."

"It's not bad once you get used to the weight," Dan lied. Dan's shoulder screamed. Dan's mind already lined up the shot.

"Or," she said with a suffocating pause, "you leave it here so you don't have to pee one-handed." Amy looking at him with those silver sunglasses, Dan's hunchback reflection staring back. "Unless you're in it for the sport."

"I'll be right back," said Dan, turning before she came up with another valid excuse. He ducked through the afternoon throng of fading tourists. All pleasantly lagging, some not paying attention at all, under the twenty-four-seven spell of that channel where everything is imaginary, even the stranger in your room at three in the morning.

The man was already bent over the sink, visor hiding him from the mirror.

Dan stood halfway across the tile floor, stuck, like a kid told to wait but not where. He squinted down his sights and stared down the barrel of his own camera over the man's shoulders. Before he pressed the red button again, he peered around the viewfinder.

Daniel hadn't looked at himself in a while. Seen himself, sure, when he brushed his straight-enough teeth and combed his thick-enough hair. But across the humid bathroom, under white-hot fluorescence, Dan looked at himself. There were more lines than he remembered and the stubble he'd been calling a vacation beard was unemployment scruff with a tan.

"Something I can do for you?" asked the man, the sink echoing it into a question from an angry god.

"Yeah, you can." Dan hid behind the camera again, zooming in, shaking. "You can stay away from my family."

The man stood up, eyes no more than beads under his visor. But Dan didn't need to see his eyes—he saw the alligator on his shirt just fine.

"Have we met?"

"I think you know me."

The man turned around. The beads narrowed.

"I don't know what you're talking about, stranger."

"Maybe if I let you hold the camera," said Dan, not as stern as he wanted, "it might come back to you."

The man smiled, not wide but still radioactive in the light. It wasn't joy, only a polite threat.

"Get that out of my face."

"I can give it to the police if you want—"

"Get that out of my face." The man, taking a step closer, making himself a lot bigger than Dan guessed across the parking lot. He was older, too.

"I don't think I will."

"That so?"

The only thing that moved was the lens, tightening up on the stranger. A granite mask squirming against the limits of auto-focus.

It took Dan two tries to say, "Stay the fuck away from my son."

"Bad word!" chirped a small voice from the handicapped stall.

"Shhh," whispered a bigger one from the same stall as two little legs dragged away from the door.

The stranger looked.

Dan stopped recording and ran.

"Did you wash your hands?" asked Amy.
　"Let's go see King Kong."
　"Way to dodge the question—"
　"C'mon."
　"Are you sweating?"
　"It's Florida."
Daniel didn't see him for the rest of the day and, far as he knew, security wasn't looking for the Taylors.

Back at the Flamingo Court, Daniel waited until Amy took her pill and passed out before he reset the chair and sat on the carpet against the door that connected rooms. Josh rolled around on their bed, working off whatever he had left, until the tourist channel put him down.

Then it was only Dan awake in Room 253 of the Flamingo Court, waiting. After the first hour, the tourist channel recycled its loop. Knights. Close-ups of steak. *What's a Wet 'n Wild?* Dan kept time by a commercial for a really big McDonald's. It always played around the 30-minute mark. Not long after the third really big McDonald's, Dan reached up over his head and unlocked the door.

Let him try.

Dan cradled the Pro Wonder in his lap, batteries as charged as they'd ever be, and straightened his back against the chintzy wood.

Let him try.

Dan fell asleep before the next really big McDonald's. When he woke up, it wasn't morning yet, but all the seams in the curtains were already glowing baby blue.

Daniel yawned and stretched against the door before reaching for the Pro Wonder that wasn't in his lap anymore.

He stood up fast enough to make his head fuzzy and scanned every surface in the room.

The Pro Wonder sat against the front door like an extra towel. Dan stepped lightly around the bed, favoring his non-stubbed toes, and studied. The chain hung limp. He couldn't remember if he set it. The deadbolt was the wrong way. He remembered that.

Thirty-one seconds gone. Dan sat at the uneven table and clicked his tongue. An involuntary metronome, ticking away his last moments of peace until the tape rewound enough. Thirty-six seconds back. A hint of bathroom, then a writhing gray void at 4:02 AM. Lines came and went, a bent rectangle maybe, with stranger shapes inside it. An eye test in an earthquake. The videographer must've been shooting something way out, hoping the auto-focus would find it in the dark. After fifteen seconds, it did.

MKK 2982. A license plate attached to a gray '92 Lumina. Dan put his hand over his mouth and watched the footage widen out to the familiar starfield of the parking lot, shot from outside this time. Pan right, slow enough to hurt, until auto-focus found the three numbers on the nearest door. 253.

The videographer lost balance again, shaking at close range, then steadied up in time to hold something in front of the lens. Another blurry rectangle, this one too close. The blurry hand fed it to a slot just over the door handle, then opened the door.

The stranger had a key.

The room disappeared in a grainy haze with only the stuttering light of the TV breaking up the black.

The stranger had a key.

The recording ended before Josh, Amy, or Daniel made cameos. The videographer didn't need to show them. He made his point, even if it was an empty threat.

As soon as it crossed Dan's overheated mind, he turned off the Pro Wonder and stared at the red RCA logo on its side for sixteen seconds. Then, for the first time that morning, Dan looked at his wife and son.

"Double Digit" Dan Taylor was one short.

"Josh?" he said, as loud as Daniel Taylor ever got. "Josh." Daniel Taylor wasn't asking anymore, bolting from the table, shoving into an empty bathroom. By the time he opened, closed, and re-opened the shower curtain, Amy was awake.

"What?" was the best she could muster.

"Somebody's messing with us."

"What?"

"It's on the tape. Somebody was in this room last night." Dan collapsed on the bed where Josh should've been, catching his head in ice-cold palms.

"What do you mean there was somebody—"

"Somebody filmed us sleeping, but I got his face on tape."

Amy bounced out of her sheets, dragging enough comforter with her to make a cigarette-scarred gown.

"What? When?"

"Yesterday at the park."

"When was he *here*?" She talked fast, not angry. Not yet.

"The last three nights. I didn't want to scare you—"

"Scare me? Scare *me*?" Dawn burned at the curtains and turned Amy's draped form into a polyester saint. "Some creep comes in here, films us sleeping, and you *hide* that from me so I'm not, what, a bummer at breakfast?"

"I didn't want it to ruin our vacation," said Daniel, calmer than he expected. So calm, Amy needed a minute.

"Don't tell me you were trying to fix this yourself." She put her hands together in mock prayer. "Please."

"I was."

The silence of a judgment long considered and now passed.

"I *did*. I *caught* him. He was outside our room and somehow got a key. It's all on there," he said, pointing at the Pro Wonder on the table. Amy followed his direction, even if she already knew what was at the end of it. "But now he took Josh."

Amy didn't scream. She didn't get as loud as she could. She turned back slowly with her entire body.

"Do they have security cameras here?" she asked.

"What? I don't know."

"Your brain is a goddamn ATM and you didn't notice if they had cameras here?"

"Amy, we don't need them—"

"*I* do." She turned away and let the comforter fall in a wrinkled pile. "Bring your tape."

She walked right out the door in her knee-length sleep shirt, barefoot.

When Daniel caught up with her, she was arguing with the woman at the front desk.

"My husband needs to see them."

"Ma'am, I do not know how our security works, that is not my area—"

"He's good with a VCR. He *is* a VCR. Let him look." She said, gesturing at the clank of empty bells on the door as Dan let it shut.

"I am sure he is, however, our security man is not in until eleven so if you could come back—"

"Thank you," said Amy, making her own invitation and walking around the counter to the only door behind it.

"Ma'am, please—"

"Somebody broke into our room last night," said Dan. "He took our son."

"Oh my god," said the woman, grabbing at her neck. "I can call the police—"

"No," said Amy. "We just need to watch."

The woman didn't pick up the phone as Daniel followed his wife. She kept holding her neck as the door closed.

As Dan expected, it was half a RadioShack squeezed into a closet. Given the recliner and mini-fridge, it must've been the break area, too. Framed in the middle of the cabled mess was a smaller, chunkier TV than in the guest rooms. It showed the parking lot, low and wide, from a camera that must've been somewhere near the lobby door. Cars and a few stray trucks blocked most of the first floor, but there was a clear shot on the second.

"Find when it happened."

"It was at 4:02 this morning—"

"Well find that."

"If they're recording in Super Long Play mode, each tape should hold six hours—"

"Rewind it then."

Dan did.

Nothing moved but the audio-visual snow, tracking lines racing up and down the image. One car came and went in reverse. Somebody sucked smoke out of the air and spit it into a cigarette on the first floor. Somebody else walked backwards out of a room on the floor above them.

"Stop. There."

Dan let it roll until the person walked in the wrong way, then pressed play.

No sound as the door opened. Dan leaned in as the intruder stepped out, hefting a white brick on one shoulder. Was his hair white? Hard to tell from the distance. No visor, obviously. No way in hell of spotting the gator on his shirt, but he could tell it was a faded shade of pink.

"It's you." Amy didn't say it like a surprise.

"No," said Dan. No other response came to mind. "No."

"You're wearing that shirt now."

Daniel already knew that, but it didn't make sense. He looked at Amy, but it didn't help.

"That can't be me," he said. He believed it, too.

Daniel believed it enough that Amy looked back at him sideways and said, almost too quietly to hear, "Watch your tape."

Dan didn't have anything else to say. He stopped the surveillance footage and replaced it with the only labeled VHS tape on the table— *Taylor Family Vacation '93.*

"Rewind until I tell you."

Past the license plate and Mr. Ed. Past the TV in the dark and the mural that said *Take Some Home.* All in living color now.

"There's only one more."

"Keep going."

Past the first intrusion.

"You promised me this tape was blank."

Past the parade, when the date twitched to 5/17/92.

"Stop," Amy said just before Josh flew out of a hotel pool. The water was bluer than Dan remembered.

"Now watch," said Amy over his shoulder.

"I've seen this." Josh laughed like a gatling gun as he threw himself back into the pool. Dan smiled, appreciating the advent of sound.

"I know. Watch it again."

"Double Digit" Dan saw memories. Amy pointing at the Epcot ball to a soundtrack of shearing wind. Josh groaning his displeasure at a purple dragon puppet.

"I don't need to see this again," said Dan as the parade started. Minnie Mouse bouncing over the crowd, fifteen-feet high if she was an inch.

"Wow," said Dan on tape, close enough for the microphone to blow out.

"I can skip to the room part—"

"No," said Amy, hand on his shoulder.

The camera drifted to the next character, still far enough away to look normal-sized. Donald Duck. Josh's favorite.

"Oh boy, here comes Donald!" said the Dan behind the camera. Zooming in, steady. Getting a great shot. "You hear that, buddy?"

The camera wilted, dipping toward the back of a hundred cheering heads.

"Josh?"

The camera lost the shot entirely, showing an edge of asphalt and a sweep of shoulder-height faces.

"Josh," Dan said, the microphone barely catching it. He realized at the same time the Dan in the Flamingo Court security office remembered.

"Josh!" as loud as Daniel Taylor ever got. "JOSH!" Louder than that as the shakes set in. The swell of brightly dressed bodies flickering by. Bumps and breezes reducing the sound to a primal roar. "JOSH!" The flurry only getting faster as Dan fought through the crowds on May 17th, 1992, the day he lost their son.

Cut to black. Almost a year to the day later. 5/18/93. Somebody holds the camera at their waist and struggles with the curtains in the Taylor hotel room. Whoever's holding the camera clicks their tongue in frustration.

Daniel stopped the tape. Sometime between the parade and the clicks, Amy left.

He hit eject, took the tape he labeled *Taylor Family Vacation '93*, and walked back to their room, past the front desk clerk who didn't say a word.

He swiped in with the keycard still in his pocket from the last recording. Awake or otherwise, Amy was already buried in her comforter. Without making too much noise, Daniel lifted the Pro Wonder from the table and took it to his separate bed. The tourist channel was still rolling on mute. He let it.

Rewinding to the beginning of his tape, Daniel lay in bed and watched the one-inch square. The Taylor family having a wonderful black-and-white time in Orlando. Seeing the sights. Rubbing elbows with Goofy. Almost dropping the camera in the hotel pool. Until somebody decided to mess with them. Luring Josh away at the parade. Breaking into the room. Following them to a theme park, threatening them in the bathroom. Before finally stealing their room key. Before kidnapping their son.

The tape ran out and Dan set it aside.

That made sense. Nobody just *lost* their kids. Not here. Not on vacation. Security, hell, *the police* would find them. "There's nothing else we can do." No. That didn't add up. What kind of man turned around once and never saw his son again?

"Double Digit" Dan Taylor closed his eyes and fell asleep to a commercial for Gatorland. For the first time in a year, he dreamed about receipts that ran on forever with numbers he couldn't read.

THE PENANGGALAN
Scott Cole

WE FLY TO PENANG, NOT having any idea what to expect when we get there.

We were supposed to spend our vacation in the Poconos, starting today, at the house Maddie's aunt and uncle own, probably sitting by the river, watching egrets and herons swoop to pinch their meals out of the water. We likely would've taken a hike at least once a day, too, but who knows what else we would've done. We were just trying to get away somewhere and couldn't afford anything too extravagant.

But then Maddie calls me at work yesterday and tells me about the crazy flight deal she's just found online, and the next thing we know, she's booking it and we're packing for a different trip, and suddenly, now, sixteen hours later, we're traveling halfway around the world for less than it would've cost us to stay in the States all week.

I can't even wrap my head around how fast it all came together. Luckily I already had the vacation time scheduled at work. I don't know how Maddie even found a place for us to stay, but she did.

Now we're sitting on the plane for I don't even know how long. Twelve hours? Fifteen? Twenty? I turn to ask her, but she's already asleep. The wheels haven't even lifted off the runway yet. I wish I could fall asleep the way she does, as quickly as she does. Sometimes I tell her she ought to get checked for narcolepsy.

So I'm sitting here without anything to do, because packing for the trip and securing a ride to the airport was such a whirlwind that I didn't even think to toss a book in my bag, and the TV screen in front of me is broken, and the WiFi on the plane isn't working well enough to load anything on my phone, so I can't even research things to do in the city we'll be touching down in tomorrow morning. I reach into the seat pocket and find the safety card and the in-flight magazine, and I also find this little booklet. It's like a journal with a black leather cover. No title on the front, but the first page inside says it's "A Field Guide to Supernatural Entities in Southeast Asia," and that seems kind of interesting. So I flip through the pages. It's full of ghosts and monsters, all sorts of things from legend and folklore. The kind of stuff I absolutely love. Halfway through, my thumb catches on a page and I'm dumbstruck. The illustration catches me off-guard. It's a beautiful woman—an angelic face with long black hair. But below the neck, she's just a mass of internal organs, hanging there like some disgusting, bloody chandelier. I'm repulsed and attracted at the same time, so I read about who she is.

"The penanggalan is a vampiric creature found in Malaysia. Typically a woman who has practiced black magic, the penanggalan soaks her body in a vat of vinegar so that she can more easily extract her organs from the shell of her outer skin. At night she floats through the air in search of victims. In Indonesia, she is called the leyak, while she is known as the manananggal in the Philippines, ahp in Cambodia, krasue in Thailand, kasu in Laos, and so on."

I've never heard of such a thing, but I'm instantly obsessed. And I'm reminded once again why Maddie and I love to travel so much. There's really nothing like seeing other parts of the world, exploring new cities, trying new foods, learning about new cultures. That's why we jumped at the chance to fly to Malaysia on a single night's notice. Well, that and the price.

Apparently I do manage to fall asleep because, the next thing I know, I'm waking up to the sound of the pilot informing us that we're making our initial descent into Penang. Maddie wakes up, too, but seems far more refreshed than I feel. Soon we're on the ground and stepping out into the hair dryer heat of the Malaysian sun. Neither of us has ever felt anything like it, and soon we're both soaked in sweat.

We take a taxi into the George Town section of Penang, where our accommodations are. It's a "guest house," whatever that means. Maddie managed to find the place last night somehow and booked the last available room, which was only possible because of someone else's last-minute cancellation.

When we arrive, the front door is locked. We ring the bell but have to wait several minutes in the blazing sun before someone answers. Finally the lock turns and the door creaks open and we enter the lobby—a small room with tile floors, a bench, a desk, and a few plants. The owner greets us, already knowing our names from the reservation. He doesn't introduce himself, though.

Maddie and I both sigh at the cooler air inside.

"Yes, we have air con," the owner says. "It's nice outside today, though. Warm, but not too hot." We both chuckle, and I secretly wonder if we're going to survive the week.

We go to our room, which is tiny, but perfectly fine, and strip off our wet clothes, then collapse onto the cool sheets of the four-poster bed. Without realizing it's happening, I instantly crash out again, and enter a dream in which I see a beautiful penanggalan zigzagging across a sheet of ice, almost like a skater, but leaving a slick trail of blood in her path as her intestines drag sloppily behind her. She smiles and stares deep into my eyes as she weaves her way toward me. Then, just as she's about to lunge in my direction, her sharp teeth bared, I'm jolted awake, and surprised to find it's now late afternoon.

"Come on, babe," Maddie says. "We didn't fly all the way here to just take naps."

I apologize and clear my eyes. In a matter of minutes, we're both up and dressed in fresh clothes and heading back out. The sun is still oppressive, but I almost feel as if I'm getting used to it already. Unless that's just wishful thinking. It probably is.

We choose a direction without looking at a map and decide to go exploring.

The sidewalks, if you can call them that, are an adventure in and of themselves. They vary in height, width, and surface type. Close attention must be paid to where each step is set down, unless you want to turn an ankle or fall into an uncovered sewer trench. Some of the walkways are covered by the awnings or roofs of shops. Others have steps or slopes. Some are in ruins; others are tiled and neatly kept. There are gaps and holes, only about half of which are covered by metal grates. Quite often there is very little space to move and two people cannot stroll casually side-by-side. We've only been walking for a few minutes and more than once we've run into clusters of motorbikes parked in the walkways, blocking foot traffic and forcing us into the streets.

The sun sets, and we're hoping for some relief from the heat, but

I imagine it will be another hour or two before we can tell a difference. We continue walking across the city, simply seeing whatever there is to see, and taking pictures without trying to look too much like a couple of clueless tourists.

The air smells fantastic—a mix of incense and street food.

Each storefront we pass appears to be a small business of some sort, and most of them are already closed for the day. We do see a man operating a small printing press inside one of them, and there is an active pizza shop with a painting on the wall of a cat wearing a Darth Vader helmet and holding a slice in one paw. We see signs for civet coffee everywhere and we discuss whether or not we want to drink something that's already run through an animal's digestive system. I'm willing; Maddie isn't.

We discover numerous examples of Penang's street art scene. One artist in particular has created a number of murals that also incorporate real-world objects. A pair of children painted on one wall "ride" the real bicycle installed in front of the building. A painted child "standing" on a real chair reaches up toward a hole in the wall, where an actual orange sits. And another painting shows a child ordering food from a street vendor, while his companion "sits" on a nearby three-dimensional bench. And so on. I spot one mural from down the street that looks like it must be a depiction of a penanggalan, and I get excited, but by the time we reach it, I realize it's just a painting of some oversized fruit.

We pass a Hindu temple and gasp at the astonishing beauty of the brightly colored sculptures piled high, towering over the street. It's a stunning sight, stacks of human and animal figures painted bright pink and blue and gold and green, all lit up with a heavenly glow against the now-dark sky.

We continue walking, and stumble upon an open-air food court. There are dozens of vendors and what must be at least a hundred tables, all surrounding a stage in the center. There's a roof, but it's held up by pillars instead of walls. A woman sings from the stage, filling the air with a language I don't understand, though I can certainly appreciate its beauty.

We decide we better eat. There's a red and yellow sign over one vendor's space advertising their Obama Vegetarian Spring Rolls, but we opt for something more traditional: the nasi lemak, a coconut rice dish. A woman comes around to take drink orders, then brings us a couple beers, and we sit and enjoy the scene for a while.

Eventually, though, the singing stops and the vendors begin closing up. We realize more time has passed than we thought, so we pack up and set out on foot once again.

Maddie asks which direction I want to head in, and I tell her in a goofy-ghoulish tone that it doesn't matter to me, as long as we keep our eyes peeled for a penanggalan.

She doesn't know what I'm talking about, and I realize I never told her about the book I found on the plane. This reminds me that I left the book behind. I had meant to hold onto it. Damn.

Then she reaches into her bag and produces a small leather-bound tome.

"Is this what you're talking about?" she asks, informing me that she grabbed it from my lap on the plane when I was asleep and it looked like it might fall to the floor.

I'm overjoyed, and I take it from her, flipping to the center of the book to find the page that features my beloved penanggalan, now the unwitting mascot of our trip. But I can't find it. Somehow it's missing from the book, even though no pages seem to have been removed. It's simply not there anymore, among the other creatures and spirits. I'm confused, but I stuff the book into my back pocket anyway and describe the strange and beautiful monster as best I can while we walk the streets without any particular destination in mind.

Maddie isn't quite as taken with the penanggalan as I am, but she's not exactly the folklore fanatic I am either. I can't help but feel that if I could show her the illustration in the book, she would understand. Maybe I just overlooked it. I'll flip through the pages again once we're back at the guest house, or we'll find the penanggalan online.

Lost in conversation, we suddenly realize we don't know exactly what part of town we're in. It certainly doesn't feature much nightlife. Soon we get our bearings and we double back in the general direction of where we're staying.

I stumble over some loose chunks of the sidewalk just as Maddie narrowly avoids falling into a trench. The same thing happens again a minute later, so we decide to detour a block over. When we turn the corner, the street opens up a bit wider. We don't encounter any people, but up ahead we see a pair of dogs resting on the sidewalk. We actually think they're statues at first, decoratively guarding a shopfront, but they stir at our approach, and we realize we need to cross the street so as not to rouse them.

That doesn't matter, though. The dogs are instantly aware of us,

and are not at all happy about our presence. Even though we've given them plenty of space, they clearly think we've intruded on their territory. They growl deeply at first, then begin barking. Maddie and I pick up our pace, speed-walking, just trying to move down the block as quickly as we can so we can find our way back in for the night. It makes no difference. The dogs bark even louder, and suddenly bolt in our direction.

I see now they're completely untethered. There are no leashes or chains, no barrier of any kind to keep them from us. We need to move.

"Run!" I say, hesitating to make sure Maddie can go ahead of me. Instead, she gives me a push on the shoulder.

"Just go!" she yells. "Don't wait for me!"

So I move, dashing as quickly as I can toward the end of the block. In the moment, I figure that if nothing else, maybe I can at least lure the dogs away from Maddie, and she can find a path to safety for herself. Once I get a certain distance away from the dogs' post, they'll surely leave me be. But for now, they're angry. And loud. And right on my heels, barking and snarling at our trespass.

I turn back to see how close they are, swearing I can feel the heat of their breath, and also needing to see if Maddie's been able to turn off somewhere. The dogs are right there, but I'm almost to the corner, so I hit the brakes and slide, the soles of my shoes scratching across the dirty pavement as I curl around the bend. I keep my balance, just barely, and make the turn. And just then, there's a loud squeal that rises up above the barking of the dogs.

The stench of vinegar pierces my nostrils, which doesn't make sense at first, until I fully round the corner. That's when I see her. Not Maddie, but *her*. Her beautiful face, her long black hair. Her dangling blood-slicked viscera.

The penanggalan.

An otherworldly light seems to illuminate her with an almost unnatural glow. She smiles at me, and I feel a warmth inside, much hotter than the heat of the Malaysian sun.

Her gaze locks onto mine, and I feel my eyes widen. The odor of vinegar hits me again, as she lunges for me, smiling, her mouth opening wide, and I see the foul cluster of internal organs—lungs, heart, stomach, intestines—hanging beneath her neck, a heap of soft, twisted entrails. So lovely. I get lost in her eyes and the black void between the rows of her pointed teeth, and she's everything to me in that moment.

I feel the bite. The smell of vinegar is overpowering. The intersection lights up, and the dogs have disappeared, and everything feels like a blooming flower. I feel a breeze, and the temperature plummets, and suddenly everything turns to red.

"I don't know," Maddie says. "It all happened so quickly. We were walking, and all of a sudden these dogs came after us. We tried to get away, but they were so fast. I told him not to wait for me, and he ran ahead, and when he turned the corner, this car just came from out of nowhere and . . ."

A woman, the driver, sits on a bench in the next room, sobbing, her tear-drenched eyes covered by her long black hair. She holds a hand firmly to her chest, just beneath her neck, in an effort to calm herself.

Down the hall, a doctor emerges and addresses a police officer.

"I've never seen anything like it before," he says. "The impact split him open like an overripe piece of fruit. The entire rib cage burst outward, and all his internal organs spilled, en masse, onto the pavement." The doctor pauses, then hands the officer a small black book. "This was in his back pocket," he says. "Maybe his wife will want it."

The officer flips the book open about halfway, to a page folded in toward the center.

"Terrible," he says, shaking his head. "But at least it was a quick death. Although I always wonder how much of what happened actually registered in the victim's mind."

He and the doctor part ways, and the officer unfolds the page in the center of the book. He is taken with the depiction of the beautiful woman there, her piercing eyes, her lovely long black hair.

He snaps the book shut and stuffs it into his back pocket, then decides to go outside for some air. As he steps through the doorway, he takes a deep breath and pauses as a warm breeze hits his face, bringing the smells of the city to his nose—incense, street food, and the slightest hint of vinegar.

SEX WITH DOLPHINS
Chad Stroup

NOT MANY MARRIAGES DISSOLVE AFTER three days.

The newly christened Kristy Gonzales, however, knows that exceptions are often prone to shoving majorities out of the way. Intoxicated vows mistakenly spoken in the presence of a Vegas Elvis, ending in annulment. The groom who cheats with one of the bridesmaids. At the reception. Or the bride who catches one of the groomsmen going down on her brand-new husband.

But it's different when a marriage ends involuntarily. There's a voracious hollowness that can never be sated, no matter how hard you try to stuff it with empty calories.

And in those rare instances when your spouse leaves you and tries to come back? Forget about it. They've become something new altogether. A unique beast.

Daniel didn't leave Kristy on purpose, though. No, that never would have happened. She knew that at the time, and she still knows it now. He was one of those mate-for-life types, like penguins or seahorses. Most people roll their eyes at such statements. They presume there's always one side pulling less weight in a long-term relationship, that there's darkness lurking behind the constant smiles shown to the public. And, in certain cases, they'd be right.

But something needs to be clarified.

"Leaving" is an inaccurate term in this instance. It implies an act performed of one's own volition. Daniel didn't leave Kristy at all. He was taken from her. Vanished in the heart of their Hawaiian honeymoon. The sea claimed him, made him one with the barnacles and the coral, nourishment for the long-forgotten creatures of the deep.

Their love, swallowed by saltwater. Perished in paradise.

Speeding down a winding two-lane road somewhere between Diamond Head and Hanauma Bay, steering a Jeep Wrangler, allowing wind to scream through her hair.

Kristy and Daniel are running away from the rest of the universe. After this honeymoon ends, Kristy has vowed to never run from anything ever again. It's the last thing she wants to do. Too many years of escaping responsibility, sidestepping reality. She's found her perfect rock and wants nothing more than to cling to it, to bring it with her everywhere she goes.

On this stretch, it's too early in the morning for the locals, too late for the less adventurous tourists who have no desire to leave the safe confines of Waikiki. But Kristy's got herself a hell of a husband, and he's scanning the coast, looking for the perfect place to stop and soak in some life. Kristy loves him so much she just might puke.

"Babe . . . pull over, pull over!" Daniel's tone seems culled from childhood. Kristy slows down, finds a safe enough spot on the side of the road to stow the Wrangler. She leaves it unlocked. It's a rental. Hands latched, they cross the road after looking both ways because life is somehow more precious when there's someone to spend it with forever.

"Why here?" Kristy asks, knowing full well Daniel's going to answer with one of his typical pseudo-profound non-answers. *Why not here?*

"Don't know," he says. Quiet enough to avoid disturbing the blissful sounds surrounding them. The wind singing. The sea dancing. "Just feels like it was calling to me, I guess."

Daniel releases his grip and darts ahead. He hops over a dented guardrail, reaches the cliff first, slips, and teeters toward the edge. Kristy shrieks, then mentally slaps herself for falling for yet another of her man's infamous pranks. His laughs are good-natured, and he keeps them going until she joins in. Then she swats him in the chest, calls him an asshole, and he grunts.

Kristy peers over the cliff's edge. The view is idyllic, a movie moment forever burned in her brain. And now she agrees with Daniel's last statement. They had no choice in the matter. This spot has chosen them.

A near-vertical drop. No stairs for convenience, but a clearly carved dirt path down the side makes for a somewhat easier trek down to the beach. The daring lovers of the past have put in the work to make it possible. Because Kristy and Daniel are young and subsisting on spontaneity and passion, they aren't yet concerned about how to climb back up. They'll find a way. They always manage.

It isn't completely private down here—a few other couples have claimed the space as well—but it's close enough. No screaming children. No sunbathing crowds. The water is such a shock of blue it's almost impossible to tell where the ocean ends and the sky begins. Within moments of their bare toes wiggling through the virgin sand, Daniel swears on his life this is the same beach featured in the famous love scene in *From Here to Eternity*. His conviction is convincing. Kristy doesn't buy it, though, and hasn't even heard of the film, but she pretends to go along with it.

The cove is a liquefied runway. Jutting from the shore is what can best be described as a hot tub formed by erosion, perfect for the two of them to intimately share. As the tide goes out, it leaves them with barely a splash of water to sit in. When the tide returns, it is magic. The water floods the roughly formed circle and rises to their chests, bringing with it all manner of aquatic life, fish with colors so east and west of the spectrum they might as well be extraterrestrial. Daniel knows the scientific names of nearly all of them. Every class, order, family, and genus. Kristy expects nothing less from a freshly graduated oceanography major, nicknamed Aquaman by his closest colleagues. A man who has spent more hours of his young adult life navigating the sea than keeping his legs secure on land.

Daniel loves the ocean and everything in it. No—"loves" is an understatement. He respects it. Believes he should have been born of its wet embrace, conceived within its depths. He'd choose to live in the salty water if his body were capable of adapting.

Her husband's affair with the sea was evident as early as their first date. And she'll never forget the bizarre conversation he instigated that evening.

"You know, dolphins are sexually confident creatures," Daniel had said mid-meal, his cheeks chipmunked with onion rings. "And here's the really weird part. There's actually people who've come clean about their attraction toward dolphins and how they've . . . uh

. . . mated with them."

Kristy had gagged so hard she'd almost spat out her quinoa burger.

"I find it fascinating," Daniel continued. "Scientifically, I mean."

She tried to hold back a wicked grin. "So what you're saying, is that if tonight turns into a second date and a third, and so on, I shouldn't be shocked if you suddenly attempt to bring some sort of Flipper fetish fantasy to the bedroom?"

Daniel kept a straight face, eyes darted off to the side, and Kristy's stomach dropped. Then he broke character, releasing his signature caw that she's since grown to adore.

"Surprised I haven't seen a viral video of one of these dolphin-lovers proposing or something," Kristy said.

"Well, dolphins aren't known to be monogamous."

"Oh, so they're like the sluts of the sea, then, huh?"

A pause. They both tried but failed to withhold their laughter.

Their fingers touched.

"I'm sure there's exceptions," Daniel said, smiling with his mysterious eyes. "Always are."

At first she'd thought herself ill for falling for a man who beamed with childlike glee when speaking about people who yearned to have sex with dolphins, but Daniel possessed many odd little quirks such as these. Never drinking soda on Sundays. Speaking openly about his personal experience with delayed puberty. Getting up to watch the sunrise to help him sleep in better. Believing *Jaws 3-D* was scarier than the first film because of how often he'd gone to SeaWorld as a child. It was these quirks (as well as her own) that had brought them closer and eventually led them here.

To Hawaii.

To this beautiful cove.

To this very moment.

They hog the hot tub-shaped rock until wrinkles form on their fingertips. The other couples give up on their turns and move on to enjoy the rest of their day elsewhere on Oahu. More heaven for Kristy and Daniel to steal for themselves. No one is willing to go to war for romance as much as newlyweds.

Daniel motions across the water to a tiny cliff. Behind it, there's an intimidating wall of rock. The cliff houses what appears to be an underwater cave, barely forty feet from where they sit and splash. Daniel grins and Kristy sees the devious child that still resides within him. Kristy grimaces and shakes her head, but the next thing she knows they are heading toward it. She wades, her feet barely touching the bottom. Daniel chooses to swim, revealing a grace he'd be hard pressed to replicate on land. A malcontent mammal who wished he were a fish, a being who yearned to split his time between both worlds.

A clawed hand here, a clutching foot there, and Daniel is atop the ledge, five feet above the surface, six at best. He flexes his arm with faux machismo and shows off the nautical star tattoo on his bicep. Kristy rolls her eyes. She's never been so happy.

Daniel hollers, "It's away!" and cannonballs into the sea. He bounces to the surface almost as quickly as he breaks it, his face beaming. "Babe, you gotta try this!" He immediately goes back for more.

Kristy shakes her head, but eventually gives in after Daniel's third jump. She wants to accompany Daniel wherever he goes, no matter how scary it gets. He extends a hand and helps her up. The surface of the rock is slick with fluorescent moss. She creeps across it with her toes curled for traction and balances herself with one hand behind her, flat against the rock wall that seems to stretch all the way to heaven. Daniel offers her a few tips on how to jump and land. She follows his advice to the exact note. Trust is everything.

Kristy flings herself off the cliff, into the water. One second she's splashing, the next her tailbone collides with solid ground. It almost knocks the wind out of her. Water rockets up her nose, and it's enough to make this a one and done experience. Her back burns. Later, when they're in the comfort of their hotel room, she plans to make puppy dog eyes at Daniel until he gives her a massage. And she'll make it worth his while, too.

Daniel goes back for more. Kristy wades back to nature's hot tub to watch. Her husband never seems to tire of jumping, and her stress is never-ending, her stomach using climbing spurs to scale her throat. Ever curious, Daniel treads water and maneuvers himself closer to the underwater cave, clinging to the slick rock at its opening.

"Hey, you're getting too close," Kristy calls out. "Be careful. There might be a current."

"Eh, it's fine." Daniel peeks into the cave as best he can, only a few inches of it visible above water. He leans in deeper and calls out a hello. A slight echo bounces back. He turns back to Kristy. "Honestly it doesn't look like it even goes anywhere."

123

He edges away from the cave, and Kristy releases a hesitant breath.

"Just one more jump and let's go, yeah?" she says. "I still wanna go check out the Dole Plantation today."

"Mmm," Daniel says, pretending to drool. "Dole Whips." He shoots her a thumbs up, climbs the side of the cliff, and leaps. The water explodes.

He doesn't come up immediately, which seems impossible. The sheer force of hitting the bottom should have pushed him right back up.

Barely a ripple on the water's surface. Kristy counts the seconds. At twenty she starts to panic.

"Hey, don't be a jerk," Kristy says, knowing he won't hear more than a muffled voice down below. The sun hits the water, blinding her with its glare. A few more seconds pass, and still no Daniel.

Kristy squints, shields her eyes with her hand. Motion in the water. Maybe.

Then his head surfaces.

"Dammit, Daniel. You had me—"

"Get out of the water!"

Without thinking, Kristy does the opposite. She leapfrogs over the edge of the hot tub and into the ocean. Frantic and splashing, Daniel goes under. She's already cursing herself, knowing she's falling for one of his lame pranks.

Daniel surfaces again, spits out saltwater. His eyes have seen the devil. "Go!" he yells. "Please! Something's got—there's something in—" And he's dragged under yet again.

She's caught Daniel in more than one innocent fib during their three years together, and she's certain his lips are telling the truth this time. She's never seen him afraid before, never knew he was even capable of such raw fear. She tries to reach toward him, but the water slows her down.

A shape moves next to Daniel, just below the surface. Something dark. More than a shadow. Something large. Long.

Daniel's body lunges backward, as if being pulled toward the cave.

Kristy screams. There's no one left on the beach to help. She dives into the shallow water. Despite it being clear enough to be bottled and sold, she sees nothing. Neither her husband, nor the ominous shape she's positive she saw.

Only the blackness of the cave. A deep, endless hole leading

124

down, down, down.

Nearly nine months later, and time couldn't have gone any slower. Isolation makes the days drag into double.

Kristy's back in Oahu. Her bank account is drained, her belly ready to burst. Maybe she hates herself more than she previously thought. Hawaii has become her personal hell, sending out a siren's call so she can kneel in front of its merciless gods and beg for . . . what, exactly? She's not getting Daniel back, so any other wish granted would bring no consolation.

She has plenty to atone for, though. *That* the gods will surely gobble up. She never knew how much sin in the guise of suffering could be squeezed into such a short period of time.

To be fair, Kristy had no clue she was carrying Daniel's child until six weeks after her husband was taken from her. Not that it mattered. She still ultimately chose moaning over mourning.

She'd planned to take care of it, thought she couldn't live with a breathing, crying reminder of everything she'd lost. At least only one of them would have to endure the resulting pain. But Kristy has lost more than she can quantify and doesn't know how much more she can bear. Too many protest lines to cross to get the outcome she thinks she wants. She deserves a medal for every day she doesn't drink herself to death.

Or she could always bathe the forthcoming child in enough secondhand alcohol to burn it, the umbilical cord an eager fuse.

She was never much of a drinker before. Practically a teetotaler. Wine at a wedding. Half a beer at a party. But she became an enemy of moderation almost the moment she stepped off the plane and set foot back in San Diego, where the sun shines three-hundred and sixty-five days a year, but only for those who have something special to live for. Otherwise the forecast is permanently dismal.

No way she'd be a fit mother. The resentment started forming in the womb immediately and only grew uglier with each passing day.

Somehow fate had allowed the fetus to thrive despite her best efforts.

And now it's almost ready to come out and play.

She's swaying on the sand in the same private cove that robbed her of her entire universe. Where countless others have no doubt enjoyed the stuff romantic dreams are made of and gone on to live the fruitful lives they expected. But, to Kristy, this place is nothing more than a gorgeous graveyard.

At least the rest of the living world has left her alone today. Being in the presence of others might force her to feel. And that racks her with dread more than anything and sends roach leg shivers down her neck. If she allows emotion into the equation, everything that's occurred becomes impossible to ignore.

Lost her cushy copywriter job. Sold nearly anything she owned that was worth a penny. All so she could return to the place where she could relive her nightmare. She tries to convince herself she came here for closure, but that's a pitiful pipe dream. The gods will never grant her closure.

They never found Daniel's body.

The Coast Guard checked the area and had her holding out hope that maybe he was just sucked under for a second and spat out the other side. Like he'd taken a ride on some crazy new waterslide and was having the time of his life. He'd surely ask Kristy to try it, tell her she'd love it, just be careful, that last dip's a doozy. But the search was just a formality.

That night, one of the officers had tried to talk to her at the station. She tuned him out. Mostly. Only bits and pieces made it past the invisible partition in her ears and into her brain, and over time she'd twisted them into painful prose that became her silent mantra.

Plenty of unexplored underwater caves on the island. Currents make them dangerous. So many tight spaces a full-grown man could get wedged into and count down his last few seconds until he takes a deep drink of the sea.

Kristy tried to explain to the officer that something had been in the water with Daniel. Attacking him. Might have been a tiger shark. But the officer crushed the idea. There hadn't been any sightings in the area recently. Plus, no blood in the water. She'd confirmed it herself. Not a drop of red staining the beautiful blue.

Back home, none of Daniel's friends could figure out how the finest swimmer any of them had ever known had suffered such a fate. Aquaman had drowned, and it shattered everything they believed in, made them atheists of logic. They attended the funeral, paid their respects, and Kristy had yet to see any of them since. For this, she was thankful.

She cried for months. Maybe the tears weren't always presented to the public—she couldn't allow herself to become a complete mess—but they poured inside with no reprieve.

Now, here, her bare feet digging into the warm sand, she only feels numbness. Better that way. The numbness keeps her alive. Keeps her living out of sheer spite.

She regrets what she's been trying to do, the monster she's become. But regret isn't enough to stop her. All she has left of Daniel are a few blurry pictures on her phone and images burned into her memory. The memories get just a little hazier with each drink she takes, each attempt at expelling the unborn.

Plenty of wine to comfort her today. A bitch to get the bottle down here, and it's far from vintage, but it'll forgive her choices the way a friend made of flesh never could. Temporarily, at least. Fitting. Forgiveness is always temporary anyway.

Kristy sits because standing is so unbearable. So is living, but she has to go on because someone needs to remember Daniel at his best and at his worst, as the wonderfully flawed man he was. His horrible taste in cinematic comedies. His secret cooking prowess. His ability to make her melt with a single cock of his head. Now he's nothing more than a name etched on a grave with no inhabitant, a name no one dares whisper anymore.

Hours pass. The wine drains. Night comes. She's done wallowing and is about to leave, but then something stirs in the water. She's been transfixed on the soothing low waves for so long that any transgression is amplified. The ripple occurs a few feet from the cave that took Daniel. Something breaks the surface. Something long and sly.

It swims toward the shore.

From the shock, from the wine, from the exhaustion of life—Kristy passes out.

Kristy always dreams of darkness.

It's been this way ever since she was a girl. No matter the scenario. Whether the dream consisted of the end of the world or the mundaneness of a day at the office, no visuals have ever come along for the ride. Only sounds. Feelings. Possibilities. A story being dictated to her.

A nagging loneliness, smothered in blackness.

Oftentimes, her dreams blur with reality. Like the time she woke up late for a test she hadn't studied for, only to realize it was Saturday and that the test was still looming in the distant Monday. This dream is no different. She's at the cove, the night after Daniel disappeared. Swapping spit with a fermented friend, not unlike tonight. The slight sound of the waves soothing her. The damp sand chafing her back, creeping into her underwear. But she shouldn't be able to feel. Not this way. Not in a dream.

Something has slithered out of the sea. A clumsy splashing, then a soggy crawl the rest of the way. Something that once walked on two legs but has spent so much time below it has forgotten how to pose as a man. But it can relearn.

A scent wafts up Kristy's nostrils. Sour brine. Overwhelming nitrogen. Her dream self wonders if the sense of smell can exist in this dimension, or perhaps if there is a sensation only present during dreaming that makes one believe they are experiencing a smell.

The deep urge, the wetness she feels down below, however, is an intimate, if not altogether welcome, friend.

She still can't see it, but she can hear it—the writhing thing from the sea. Inching toward her like a pathetic worm, chittering with glee. It pauses just before reaching her, as if awaiting consent, but nature does not wait for the world. It exists to create.

The creature slides on top of her, an oppressive weight. It whispers in her ear, in words that take time to make sense.

And then they do. Words so sweet. So familiar.

And she remembers that some dreams aren't dreams at all.

They are memories.

She should have known all those months ago when she'd awoken on the beach, dawn tearing away night's heavy curtain. Waiting for Daniel to quit it with his joke. Her mouth filled with sand. Drenched in slime and the stench of day-old seafood. So stupid. She'd fooled herself into thinking she'd vomited all over herself. A typical night for the lonely lush.

But she didn't notice something was off until she was a week late. Could have been a fluke. Wouldn't be the first time she'd had a scare. But then a couple of weeks later she got sick. The kind of sick where you just know.

She'd lived through a few regrettable nights since Daniel's disappearance. So much liquid courage and so little pride that she couldn't recall the names of the men she allowed to use her, much less their faces or the circumference of their pathetic cocks. She remembered Daniel mentioning something about dolphins, that the females would often mate with multiple partners during estrus. Maybe this was just her fucked up way of honoring his interests.

A close call or two, but not enough to teach her a lesson. At first she was certain the child inside her had to be the result of one of those encounters taken to its extreme. To its most likely outcome.

Except once she felt the growing being stir within, she understood what it really was.

A gift.

And who had given it to her.

And when.

Now—it's the second night of her return trip to Oahu. Perhaps the third. She's lost track. Once she arrives at the cove again, she doesn't have to wait long. Because she knew to come at dusk. Just as the cove once called to Daniel, now it beckons her.

Redemption's a real thing, almost tangible.

Maybe she'll make a decent mother after all. Hard to say, since the rules are about to change significantly.

The moonlight shines a pathway on the water. Moments later, it emerges.

He emerges.

An evolution of the man he once was. The man he no longer is.

Her Daniel.

Always here, waiting for her.

Even after the night Kristy felt him inside her and—deep down, despite such drastic changes—recognized him, she still didn't believe it was him. Dreams can be tricky that way. Especially when they're not dreams at all.

Except tonight the details are crystal. The nautical star on the area that had once been his arm, now faded and blending into the smooth, rubbery, gray flesh. His face elongated and smoothed to a point, his head bald and domed, his smiling teeth tiny and plentiful and perfectly sharp, his body a shimmering wet wonder.

And—even though they've shifted to the sides of his head—it's the eyes that sell it.

Those mysterious, laughing eyes.

She wades into the water. Once her belly feels the shock of cold, the baby kicks inside her. It's ready.

But she's not sure if *she's* ready.

She takes Daniel's hand. Fin. Flipper. Something new altogether that nature has failed to share with the rest of the world.

There are others like him waiting in the water, a protective semicircle, their faces barely breaking the surface. The ones who changed him. Who gave him his true purpose. Kristy forgives them.

Sympathizes. They made choices, however long ago, and now she must make hers.

They've come to congratulate her. To welcome her to the family. And she knows it's time for a change.

The new Daniel guides her toward the cave. They're going where she should have followed so long ago. To finish their honeymoon. Gently, he tries to push her under, but she hesitates. She's shivering. Fear, anticipation, ecstasy, what's the difference? He whispers in her ear, the echolocation making perfect sense. She understands his intent. Everything will be just fine. She'll be safe down below. He won't let her drown. He'll teach her to breathe.

His fin nudges her again. She sucks in a deep breath, and then she allows it.

Trust is everything.

CAUGHT A GLIMPSE
Patrick Lacey

HE WATCHED HER THROUGH THE window.

He hadn't meant to. He'd meant to brush his teeth, wash his face, and browse Netflix on the creaking bed until he drifted asleep. But he'd lingered in the bathroom, counting the gray hairs in his stubble and the lack of any on his head. He had been thinking about what he might look like this time next summer, and the one after, when he'd spotted something in his periphery.

The cottage was one in a line of six, all identical save for their colors, his yellow, hers green. The bathroom window faced his neighbor's courtyard and in the courtyard, sitting at the patio table, was the woman. Turned away, smoking and reading by the glow of the flood light.

Alan thought he was alone here. He'd chosen this spot to gather his thoughts and get some sleep. No screaming kids. No cartoons. Just the lapping of waves and swaying of the trees.

The woman must have had the same idea.

She puffed her cigarette and patted away the ashes. They missed the tray and the breeze took them. She could see him if she turned the slightest. The shade's slats were open, the bathroom light on, and Alan's peering eyes would be the first thing she spotted. He flicked the switch and closed the blinds, but he couldn't help himself from lifting one slat and taking another look.

With the light gone, he had a better view and he saw now that she wasn't wearing a shirt. His face grew flush, like he'd been caught stealing, but instead of closing the slat, he opened it wider. Her hair was black, on the verge of blue. She flipped the page of her book every fifteen seconds or so. A speed reader. When she did turn around, to crush her cigarette, he noticed two things. Three, really. The first and second were her breasts. The third was her sunglasses. They looked cheaply made, something you could win at the arcades at the boardwalk, and he wondered why she should wear them this late, pushing midnight, and how she could read through them. How she could see much of anything.

She stood, cracked her neck, and peered toward Alan's cottage.

Toward Alan.

He closed the slat and tried to catch his breath, thinking there'd be a knock at the door.

The cops.

Sir, we received a complaint from the woman next door. Know anything about that?

They'd shove him into the back of a cruiser. Try explaining *that* to Tanya.

Or maybe she hadn't seen him. Maybe he'd open the slat once more and prove to himself she was sitting again, speed reading through her cheap shades. He hesitated, index finger on the brink, before he lifted the plastic.

The patio was empty. The book lay page down, open to where she'd left off. The ashtray still held her crumpled cigarette. The flame hadn't yet died. A faint ember glowed, smoked.

Her sunglasses rested on the table, too, and for some reason he couldn't pinpoint, he didn't like the idea of her eyes exposed.

The breeze picked up, blowing smoke toward the window.

He stopped watching after that.

In the morning, he managed to forget about it in the way you push aside a nightmare. You wake and yawn and you brew your coffee like normal. It doesn't hit you until later, as you're buttering your toast or showering—or in Alan's case, as he was about to go for his daily jog.

Hand on the knob, he remembered. He tensed, again certain she'd spotted him. But he hadn't done anything wrong, not technically speaking. He'd closed the blinds and maybe he'd lingered for a free show, but he was only human.

He locked the door behind him and jogged to the left, toward the beaches and tourist shops and away from her cottage. He passed a few people along the way, mostly locals and retirees. A few college kids emerged from doorways, their eyes red and swollen.

He turned toward the beach and stopped for a breather on the first bench. He'd need to take it slow going back. Tanya would be proud. She liked to remind him he wasn't getting any younger, like he hadn't noticed, but in a strange way *she* wasn't getting any *older*. She was ten years his junior. In their decade and a half together, he'd packed on twenty pounds and had started an impressive collection of wrinkles. But she'd stayed the same. He'd put it to the test before by taking a picture of their first anniversary and comparing it to their last. And though she didn't agree, Alan was convinced Tanya hadn't aged a moment.

He should've brought her here. Shouldn't have told her this was a work trip even if it was a half-truth. He did have meetings and presentations, and he did have calls with clients, but they would each be held remotely. He could've done them at home in his office, or he could have done them here with Tanya and the kids.

The breeze picked up. It chilled him.

He jogged back at half the speed and stopped at the convenience store across from his cottage. There was a deli counter near the back, run by a man with arthritic hands and ghost-white hair.

Don't laugh. At least he's got some.

And besides, he made one hell of a breakfast burrito.

Alan grabbed a cup and lid at the coffee station and reached for the cream in the fridge.

In the door's reflection he saw her standing there. Standing just outside of the store. A group of construction workers passed by, soaking her in before they stepped inside, but she made no effort to move. Instead, she stared.

Stared at him.

At least it felt that way. It felt as though she'd come across the street to confront him and it didn't matter if he waited her out.

"Order up," the ancient man called from behind the counter.

Alan nearly dropped the cream. He poured too much into his cup. It would be cold now, and too sweet, but he didn't much care. He paid for the burrito. The juices soaked through the wax paper, dripping down his fingers, and the eggs and cheddar smelled like garbage.

When he passed the doors, pausing to browse the magazines and newspapers, he saw the construction workers and no one else.

The girl was gone.

"You going or what?" the closest of the workers said.

He gulped. "After you."

His phone rang.

Tanya.

He ought to call her back when his stomach settled. The burrito had turned to shrapnel in his gut. The coffee hadn't done him any favors either. He'd taken two Tums but still his abdomen gurgled. He didn't want to worry Tanya. He'd already lied.

He stood in front of the living room wall, beneath the lighthouse painting. The only spot that could pass for a hotel room.

He answered. "Hi, sweetie."

"Hi, honey. How's everything going?"

"Good. Boring as hell but good. Been on the phone all day and the food here sucks. My stomach's shot."

"You don't sound good. Sure you're not coming down with something?"

"Just a bad burrito." His stomach churned once more, the pain deeper this time, and he wondered if she might be onto something. Food poisoning or worse.

"What was that?"

He shook his head. "I didn't say anything. Must be my stomach." He paced to get his mind off the pain before he remembered he was in a cottage on Martha's Vineyard, not a hotel in the city. "How's everything with you?" he asked, hoping she hadn't noticed.

Before she could answer, something crashed in the background, and he could hear her chiding Lisa and Eric, both in their terrible twos, both wonderful pains in the asses. Twins in his forties. He hadn't slept in years. Part of the reason he'd come here. Most of the reason.

"They keeping you busy?" he asked, thinking he could've been there helping her, thinking they could've shared a family vacation.

She dropped the phone and promised a time out. Suddenly the twins grew quiet. "They're fine. Everything's fine." Another of her talents, not just bypassing the aging process but never admitting her exhaustion or frustration. A talented woman, his wife. "What did you say?"

He frowned. "Nothing. I didn't say anything."

"Sounds like there's voices. Are you guys sharing a drink or something?"

He looked around the cottage. The *empty* cottage. "Must be static. Reception here is shit."

"You're breaking up."

He told her he'd call later. Tell the kids he loved them. He wasn't sure if she'd heard him. He hung up and froze because for a moment he could hear them, too. The voices. Whispering. Words too soft to make out. Words that seemed to come not from outside but all around him.

The doorbell rang.

He dropped the phone. Better be good. He'd had enough excitement. He opened the door.

It was the girl.

"I'm sorry," he said, sweating again now.

She cocked her head. "Sorry for what?"

He paused, smiled, shook his head. "Sorry for not answering sooner."

She held up a mug. "You don't have any sugar, do you? Please say you do."

She wore her sunglasses and, even in the late-morning light, he couldn't detect her eyes behind the plastic. Not the irises or the whites and certainly not the pupils. He wondered why just as she cleared her throat and raised the mug higher.

"Right," he said, heading for the cabinets. "I don't live here." He opened the first. Empty save for some water-stained tumblers.

"No one lives here. All rentals."

He opened the next one. Chipped plates and a can of condensed soup long since expired.

"But they usually stock these places, you know?" she said. "And I've got a migraine. A *fucking* migraine to be exact. So I figured maybe you could save me a trip to the store."

That was it. The glasses. Migraines. Of course.

He opened the third cabinet and there was the sugar, a jar of packets. One had torn open and spilled white crystals to the bottom. "Here," he said.

"I only need a couple. I don't really care about the taste, as long as I can get it down."

But he handed her the jar anyway, insisting, and she thanked him,

135

saying she owed him one. On her way down the front steps, she paused. "Hey."

"Yeah?" He wiped away sweat but he couldn't keep up.

"You might want to close your bathroom blinds. I can see right into your window."

The first video conference was a bust. Seven of ten attendees bailed and John McKinley bowed out early, blaming technical difficulties and not the meet-up with his kid's Algebra teacher. Only Alan and Terrence Gardner remained. Terrence worked for Alan's sister company, in a near identical position, and they often talked shop. Mostly gossip and wondering which of their managers would have a nervous breakdown first. Close race.

"You look like shit," Terrence said.

"You sound like my wife." Alan scratched his scalp. He'd broken out in a rash. He'd tried lotion and a warm cloth but to no avail. Allergies probably. Something in the air. And he couldn't argue with Terrence. He saw his reflection in the chat window. Dark bags beneath his eyes, both swollen.

"You've been working too hard," Terrence said. "What you need is a beer or five."

"Now you're making sense." He stood and grabbed a bottle from the fridge, popped the top with his car key. He took a long swig and belched. One of the benefits of telecommuting.

Terrence raised his own drink into the frame, what looked like three shots of whiskey and not much else. "Like I was saying, Sheila's been on my back. More than usual, I mean. She's asking for spreadsheets on top of spreadsheets and I'm about to lose my mind. You know what she does with them? Nothing. Lets them sit in her folder."

Alan peered toward the bathroom. He heard something. A hissing noise. It was dark in there. He hadn't turned on the light since last night. The door was halfway open. He couldn't see the window or anything else that might have been inside.

"Earth to Alan."

He stood and walked toward the darkness, not because he wanted to but because of the sound. Not hissing at all, he realized with a few steps, but water. Running water. He approached the slats like they might bite if he wasn't careful. His finger hovered for a while before he risked a glance.

The outdoor shower was running and she was there under its

stream. He shouldn't watch for plenty of reasons, yet it felt comfortable to stay like that. She lathered her hair. He studied the tattoo on her shoulder among other things. A pentagram or something similar. Metal head maybe.

Whoever had built the cottages had not taken privacy into consideration. A half-wall separated the shower stall from the patio and the street beyond, but the bathroom window left nothing to the imagination.

Stop watching, he thought, and this time it wasn't just guilt or shame. It was something else, like his burning gut knew something he didn't.

The girl rinsed her hair and turned around. He now saw she was still wearing her glasses.

Her sunglasses.

"Alan," someone called from the kitchen table. "Alan, everything okay?"

Terrence.

He shook his head and stepped back to the computer. "Yeah, fine. Had to take a leak." He took another swig of his beer. It tasted sour.

"Thought you said Tanya wasn't with you."

"She's not. She's watching the kids for the weekend. And don't get on me about it. I feel awful as it is."

Terrence paused. He swirled his drink, ice cubes clinking against the glass. "You fucking with me?"

"Fucking with you how?"

Terrence peered through the screen, past Alan, like he could lean forward and step out of the laptop. "Fucking with me as in I just saw someone walk through the living room."

Alan forced a smile and waited for the punchline. "What'd she look like?"

"You better not be getting something on the side. And what kind of girl wears sunglasses inside?"

The next morning, Alan woke to knocking.

He opened the door a few inches. The light was hangover bright but he'd only managed half his beer before dumping the rest.

"What?" he said.

The girl held up the jar. "Thought I'd give this back to you."

"I said you could keep it."

She smirked and, though he still couldn't see her eyes, he had the sense they didn't agree with her lips. Her eyes weren't smiling. "Yeah but it's not really yours, is it?"

He shrugged. "What do I care? No one's gonna notice a missing jar."

"Grumpy today, are we?"

He opened the door and stepped outside. The morning air was frigid and he wore only boxers and slippers. "Are you playing some sort of game with me?"

"Game?" She didn't step back when he stepped forward.

"Answer the question. Did you come into my cottage last night?"

She covered her mouth. "You're joking."

He wasn't.

"I think I'm gonna get going," she said, but before she turned, her glasses slipped down the crown of her nose. No more than half an inch but more than enough. He could see her eyelids and the faint suggestion of something else. Something black and swirling, a storm cloud in the darkest portion of the night, so dark you can't tell if you're sleeping, if you might jolt awake at any moment.

The rash along his scalp came alive with crawling things and his stomach filled again with needles. He tasted bile and yesterday's beer.

Alan shook his head. The girl was at the bottom of his walkway. He hadn't seen her move. She'd pulled her glasses back up.

"Thanks again for the sugar," she said.

He heaved into the toilet, wiped his mouth with the hand towel, and didn't bother showering. His suitcase lay half open on the couch. He tossed his clothes inside without folding and forced his laptop into the mess. The zipper wouldn't close, but that was fine. No time to be picky. No time for anything but getting the fuck out of here.

He dialed Tanya. She answered on the first ring.

"Alan? Jesus, is everything okay?"

"I'm fine, why?"

"You said you'd call."

He checked his watch. It was barely nine. "I was going to this morning."

"You said you'd call *yesterday* morning."

"What're you getting at?" But he'd already pulled his phone from his ear and had seen the date. A day. He'd lost a full day. Missed three meetings and a seminar, and hopefully nothing else.

"Daddy?"

Tim, grabbing the phone from his mom while Tanya protested in the background. "Daddy, when are you coming home?"

"Now, buddy. I'm leaving now. Listen, tell your mother I'm sorry and that I'll be home this evening and tell her we're going on a vacation next week. I don't care where as long as it's not this cottage or the one next to it. Tell her—"

The line went dead.

His screen was black even though he'd left the phone charging overnight. Or maybe that was the night before.

He reached for the suitcase when the sound came again.

The hissing sound that wasn't a snake, though in the end it wasn't all that different. He did not want to follow the sound into the dark bathroom. The air was dank and stale and he hadn't flushed his vomit. Yet he found himself walking again in that direction. Found himself wiping tears from his tired eyes but at least he *had* eyes.

The girl was out there again, standing beneath the spray. She faced the bathroom window this time. The blinds had been lifted. He didn't remember doing that either.

"Why don't you meet me over here, Alan?"

"I didn't tell you my name," he said.

"You didn't have to."

He left the bathroom and the cottage and even though his car keys were in his back pocket and even though the driver's side door was within reaching distance, he passed through the driveway and onto the sidewalk. Her front door was unlocked.

Inside it was too dark, like the windows had been painted over with black. Faint light lay in the distance and along his way he saw things in the shadows. Misshapen things. The floor was sticky in some places, wet in others. He smelled something sweet, metallic even. And were those candles burning, and was that a book in the center of them, on the floor, the book she'd been reading that first night? Was that a symbol etched into the wooden boards, the same one inked onto her shoulder?

By the time he stepped outside, she'd finished her shower and was drying off with a towel adorned with sunflowers. Her hair fell in damp clumps. "Have a seat," she said, pointing to the patio table.

He nodded and sat and it was hard to speak, like his lips had grown numb or belonged to someone else.

"Smoke?" she said.

He shook his head but she gave him one anyway. He'd quit years ago, just before the twins, and Tanya would kill him if she knew. She set the filter onto his lips.

"You've been watching me," the girl said.

He tried to shake his head once more but even that was a struggle.

"It's fine," she said, lighting a cigarette for herself. She pulled on a pair of underwear and a bra, colors mismatching, and sat across from him. She blew a cloud of smoke his way and, in the mist, she wasn't the girl at all. Wasn't any girl. But once the smoke cleared, he saw her olive skin and sunglasses again.

"I guess I've been watching you, too. We both came here for the same reasons. Peace and quiet. To not be bothered. Tell me I'm wrong."

The cigarette fell from his mouth. She set it into the ashtray.

"But there's no such thing as peace or quiet, not truly. You must agree. Two kids. Twins, born minutes apart. Both of them just as loud and they've taken to saying *shit* even if you insist you never swear in front of them. You're tired, Alan. You shouldn't feel guilty about this, about wanting to get away. You're an honorable man. Tanya knows that. It's not like you're cheating either. You took a few peeks. All men are pigs. But even if I offered myself to you right now, let you fuck me on this table, you wouldn't. And that's the part I hate. It makes this harder."

"May wha hodder?" he said, tongue swollen in the center of his mouth.

"This." She took a deep drag of her cigarette and instead of putting it out in the ashtray, she removed her glasses and placed it where her left eye should have been. The cavity swallowed it, filter and all, and he could see one last stream of smoke before it fell into wherever the opening led.

"In case you couldn't tell," the girl said, "I'm not from around here. I'm not from anywhere you would know on a map or could pronounce with any word you've ever known. And I'm tired too, Alan. Believe you me."

More and more he watched the swirling in her eyes. More and more there was nothing else.

"I'm at a crossroads. I came here to get away, to pretend I'm flesh and bones like the rest of you and for a while it worked. But you caught a glimpse. Saw through the magic trick. So now it's a tough choice. Do I let you go and ponder what you've seen, let it keep you up for most nights when you're already so tired?"

She leaned closer to him. He could feel the pull of the blackness, could smell the cigarette wafting up and countless other things, too. Some, sweet like nectar. Others, rotten like carrion.

"Or do I make sure you never tell anyone about this? Because if you do, there will be consequences. I take my orders from higher up, too, you know. We all have managers."

He heard the hissing sound again and realized it wasn't the shower this time but a river, a river running somewhere inside of her. And there were voices, too. Screaming, though whether from pain or pleasure, he couldn't tell. Not yet.

"There is a third option, Alan. One where we can both walk away."

He thought he nodded, but he wasn't sure.

"Would you like that? Would you like to walk away from this with more knowledge than any man should ever know?"

Sometimes the screams layered over one another, a symphony, and it was beautiful and horrible. The hole was getting larger. Her eyes were pulling him toward them.

"You want to know, don't you?" the girl asked. "You want to know what's in there."

Don't nod, some part of him said. *Whatever this is, whatever she's about to show you, it's not just knowledge.*

But that part of him was a whisper now, amongst the screams, and he'd already managed a single numb-tongued syllable.

"Yes."

The girl smiled and, this time, even without her eyes, he could tell she meant it.

He woke again on the cottage floor. He scrambled to find his phone, to see how much time had passed, but he saw it was only an hour later. Same day, same week. Still time to leave.

He stood with some effort. The room circled him, like he'd been placed in the middle of a carousel. His suitcase lay where he'd left it. He tapped his back pocket, felt the keys.

From here, he could see the bathroom. The blinds were still up but the patio was empty. Even the ashtray was gone. She'd drugged him and she hadn't taken his money or laptop, but she hadn't spared him either. He caught his reflection in the mirror.

His phone rang, buzzing along the kitchen counter or the floor or wherever he'd left it, but the sound was miles away now. No chance of him ever finding it and telling Tanya he was on the way.

He studied himself, counting the gray hairs in his stubble and the lack of any on his head. He thought about what he might look like this time next summer, and the one after.

And he grabbed onto the sunglasses for only a moment before he slipped them off and saw just what she'd taken.

IN THE WATER
Mark Wheaton

"WOW, THAT'S BEAUTIFUL! TAKE MY picture!"

Candice handed her camera to Jenn and leaned as far back over the boat's guardrail as gravity would allow. The resort's sailboat sliced through the water at a good twenty knots. It had picked up the tail end of the fall's monsoon winds blowing down the Thai coast through the Straits of Malacca.

Jenn planted her foot against a deck cleat and snapped a few pictures. The water was calmer closer to shore, and photos easier. But out in open water, the waves slapping into the hull sent up a sheet of spray and it made for a more dramatic backdrop.

"Did you get it?" Candice asked, voice lilting up as fear crept in.

"All good!" Jenn said.

Candice steadied herself as the boat bounced over a high swell. She spun around, grabbing for the jib boom, only to miss and land on her hands and knees. She slid toward the edge of the deck. The captain's words of warning of how long it would take to slow and turn the ship, should someone tumble off, echoed in her mind.

One of the boat's assistant cooks lunged forward to take her arm, steadying her as she regained her balance.

"Thank you," Candice said. "Shouldn't have had a second Mai Tai before getting on board!"

The assistant cook, Thinh, laughed amiably.

"No problem," he said.

"Special Agents Rucker and Attenberg have arrived."

Sub-Lieutenant Wichan Pimdee closed his eyes and tented his fingers over the bridge of his nose. There wasn't enough Ativan on the island of Phuket to prepare his mind for what would next follow his corporal through the office door.

"Show them in, please," Pimdee said, getting to his feet.

It was only 80 degrees Fahrenheit outside but sweat had already saturated Pimdee's shirt. On a normal day, he wouldn't mind. He'd go for a swim on his way home or after he picked up his kids from school. But when greeting members of foreign law enforcement, he knew how much his appearance factored into the level of condescension he'd receive.

The first American who entered was a pink-faced hulk of a man with a tight buzz cut and hair the color of wheat. His neck was so large it looked like his shirt collar might burst. He was followed by a middle-aged woman who looked exactly one-quarter his size with a wild nest of curly brown hair atop her head and thick-framed glasses.

"Agent Attenberg," Pimdee said, extending a hand to the woman. "We spoke on the phone."

"Sub-Lieutenant Pimdee," she said. "This is Agent Rucker."

Pimdee forced a smile and shook the beefy man's hand. He'd expected some sort of iron grip in return, the sign of a true American cowboy, but the man's palm was so sweaty it was like shaking hands with an eel.

"Welcome to Phuket," Pimdee said. "Is it your first visit to Thailand?"

Attenberg stared at the young sub-lieutenant as if taking his measure. Her gaze flicked away and returned, betraying a hint of irritation.

"I'm sorry, but can we go straight to the crime scene?" she asked. "I have two sets of parents back in Boston, desperate for answers. Every second we waste on pleasantries compounds their frustration."

"Of course," Pimdee said, signaling his corporal to bring around a Jeep.

The water glowed turquoise a dozen feet off port bow. Everyone on deck went quiet. Jenn lifted her camera. The patch of light blue, a ring of white around its edge, grew larger.

"Oh my God!" Candice exclaimed as the whale surfaced and

spouted. "That's amazing!"

A second, smaller turquoise spot appeared next to the larger whale.

"That's the baby," the resort's guide, who'd introduced himself as Thinh, said in English before switching to Mandarin and repeating for the other tourists aboard.

It surfaced next to its mother, sending a thin jet of white spray into the air. The handful of tourists on deck, some still finishing the lunch laid out by the crew, applauded.

"How old is it?" Jenn asked.

"Very young," Thinh said. "Maybe a week or two. They're born already at 2,000 pounds and about twelve feet long."

"Wow," Jenn said, switching to video.

As soon as the whale had been sighted, the sails were hauled down to avoid the boat striking the animal. Now, as it bobbed idly up and down in the water, the whales seemed intrigued.

"Are those birds?" Candice asked, pointing to flashes of silver splashing over the water ahead of them.

"Flying fish," Thinh said. "Fleeing the whales."

The whales glided forward, not sharing in their prey's panic. Candice watched the fish go, springing from the gentle waves as if trying to escape a patch of boiling water. The sky off the boat's starboard side was much darker, blue purpling almost to black, like an atmospheric bruise.

"Is that a storm?" Jenn asked.

But Thinh had gone back below deck.

"Is it going to rain?" Candice asked, forlorn. "There goes our beach day."

Only the corpses had been removed. The rest of the suite was exactly as it had been thirty-six hours earlier when resort security officers had forced the door, tearing free the long strips of plastic supergluing it shut. These same strips were glued in place around each of the windows and doors, even the one leading into a closet.

Pimdee thought the smell, which had sent the security officers staggering back into the hall, had dissipated slightly.

"No guest reported an odor?" Agent Attenberg, wearing a hooded hazmat suit with shoe covers, asked as she stepped around the scene.

"Nothing," Pimdee said. "After the fact, the guests in the room next door reported hearing noises, but no smells."

"The other side of that wall or that one?" Attenberg asked, first pointing to the wall of the living room and then to the bedroom.

"Bedroom side. Where we found the bodies. We think they sealed themselves in the suite first. Then the bedroom. Then the closet itself."

Agent Rucker headed for the bedroom, slipping on the plastic sheet which covered a section of the floor. Attenberg pointed up to the constellation of pinhead-sized blood stains splattered across the ceiling and down the ocean-facing windows.

"Have you determined whose blood that is?" she asked.

"Not yet. We sent samples to our new regional forensic science center in Yala, but also to your people at Quantico, as well as the PNP crime lab in Manila."

"Why Manila?" Rucker asked from the bedroom.

"Justo Arevalo and Tito Canoy were both Filipino nationals," Pimdee explained. "Their families have petitioned their government to investigate as well."

Agent Rucker scoffed. Pimdee said nothing.

"Where were the samples taken?" Attenberg asked.

"Carpet, walls, windows, bedsheets, multiple shower curtains and towels, bathroom tiling, and furniture," Pimdee said.

"Do you have any concerns the bodies were moved postmortem?"

"Yes, it's clear Arevalo and Canoy—"

"I mean, the victims," Attenberg said.

"You're referring to Candice Burton and Jenn Schlosser as the victims?" Pimdee asked.

"Of course, they're the victims," Rucker said, storming out of the bedroom, his face a few degrees pinker than before. "You thought we meant the guys trying to kidnap them?"

"We're still assessing the situation," Pimdee said, staring back at the angry American. "To your eyes, they're victims. To mine, I'm unable to make that determination, particularly as their bodies were in such an advanced stage of decomposition."

Rucker scoffed.

"You're telling me you've got a couple of pretty young American girls here in one of the world's number one destinations for sex tourism *and* traffickers—when they turn up not just dead but glued into a pair of plastic cocoons in what's obviously a kidnapping gone bad, you're open to the possibility they're the perpetrators? That they killed these two men, sprayed blood everywhere, high-fived, then zipped themselves into the bags to suffocate and die? Only to be discovered when their bodies practically explode and drip fluid into the laundry room below?"

Pimdee looked from Rucker to Attenberg, then sighed.

"What I know for certain is Arevalo and Canoy died in the evening of the 15th not long after they can both be seen entering this suite in the hallway's security footage," the sub-lieutenant said. "Our preliminary autopsy has their times of death right around seven o'clock. Our witnesses reported hearing both Burton and Schlosser conversing at least five hours beyond this point as late as one in the morning."

"The fluid was noticed when?" Attenberg asked.

"On the morning of the 17th."

"The Filipinos weren't missed?"

"They were only sent to check on the refrigerator," Pimdee explained. "The sensors inside showed it had been emptied completely, which would spark a bill of $500. Add that housekeeping had been verbally refused for two days straight and a welfare check was proposed."

"Doesn't answer the question," Attenberg pressed. "What happened when the two men didn't show up to their next shift?"

"It is my understanding calls were made to their houses and cell phones, but there was no answer."

"That doesn't seem suspicious?" Rucker demanded.

"Not under the circumstances," Pimdee admitted.

"What circumstances?" Rucker asked.

"The storm," Pimdee replied simply.

"Of course," Attenberg said. "The storm."

By the time the sailboat returned to the pier jutting out from the resort's private beach, the decision had been made for the crew to drop off the passengers then resume sailing around to the more protected, western coast of the land. A line of workers waited on the dock, umbrellas in hand to escort the guests through the light rain.

Jenn and Candice waited for the older tourists to disembark, the latter staring wistfully down the long beach as workers collapsed cabanas and hauled in chairs and umbrellas in preparation for the coming storm. Closer to the hotel, wait staff brought in tables, chairs, and heating lamps from the outside dining areas.

"I can't believe it!" Candice moaned. "The whole place is on lockdown. What're we supposed to do?"

"There's a shuttle into Phuket City," Jenn said. "It's on the western side, right?"

"Unfortunately, they cancel shuttle service for storms," Thinh said, helping them step from the boat. "The roads flood and power lines come down. It's dangerous."

"Is it best to hole up in our rooms?" Candice asked.

"Only if you want to miss the party," Thinh said. "While some workers go to their homes to be with their families, others do stay at the resort. The grand ballroom is perfectly safe. The windows can withstand hurricane winds. This is but a storm. Generators are run. Fires lit in the fireplaces. There's an open bar. Anything that might spoil in the kitchen refrigerators is brought out for a feast. There's music and dancing. All inches away from this great and beautiful calamity."

That *does* sound fun, Jenn thought.

They headed into the resort, crossing the sand then ascending the marble steps leading to the backdoors of the main lobby. They thanked their umbrella-wielding escorts and ducked inside. If there was a lot of activity on the beach, there was twice as much in the lobby. Desk clerks juggled phones. The wait staff set up long tables and laid out warming trays. Cases of liquor were wheeled in on dollies, prompting cheers from a handful of guests.

A cart of bullhorns and first aid kits arrived as well. Jenn noticed they were quickly hidden in a luggage storage closet.

The hotel was being prepared for disaster, but the excitement was palpable.

"Everybody'll flip when they hear about this," Jenn said.

Candice's gaze fell on a tall, deeply tanned young man wearing flip-flops and board shorts, his upper torso and arms covered in colorful tattoos.

"Jenn, it's the guy from Goa!" Candice said, leaning in. "What was his name again? Jasper-something?"

"Bacevich," Jenn said, though she wasn't looking at the apparently ever-shirtless Tasmanian, but instead at the young woman they'd initially mistaken for his girlfriend beside him, Tamara.

But you can call me Tama.

Tama seemed to notice Jenn at the same moment. Her face lit up and, suddenly, there was a gorgeous, green-eyed young woman in a bikini top and shorts racing straight for Jenn, arms outstretched.

"Jenny!" Tama cried. "Candy!"

Tama's arms encircled her neck to pull her in for two kisses on the cheek, a third on the nose.

"I can't believe it's you!" Tama said.

When Tama kissed Jenn a fourth time, this one grazing her lips, the explosion of endorphins inside Jenn's head somehow drowned out the screams around her as a door blew open, sending a pair of planters crashing to the floor. The electricity went out a second later and the ballroom was plunged into semi-darkness.

Jenn barely noticed.

The video footage blinked from the fourth kiss to white noise.

"That's when the power dropped?" Agent Rucker asked.

Pimdee avoided making a snarky comment about the agent's deductive powers and nodded.

"That's the last time we have eyes on them?" Agent Attenberg asked.

"Cameras, yes, but we have eyewitnesses, both guests and staff, who saw them throughout the night," Pimdee said.

Both agents went silent, confirming to Pimdee the Americans would treat these testimonies as anecdotal at best. In this case, he agreed. Not only due to the storm, but also because a third of the witnesses had misidentified the Americans when shown photos.

Attenberg rewound the footage, freezing it on Jasper and Tama.

"These two are still missing?" she asked.

"They are," Pimdee confirmed.

"Have you notified their parents? They're brother and sister, right?"

"While that's what their travelogues and social media profiles claim," Pimdee said, "they're actually not. They're not even from Tasmania but likely Ecuador. In our search, we've had them appear at other resorts under an array of aliases even checking in with EU and South African passports."

"Have you reached out to Interpol?" Attenberg asked.

"Yes, we're expecting a reply soon. But the reality is they could be miles from here by now."

Attenberg scrutinized Pimdee's face.

"You don't believe that, do you, Sub-Lieutenant?"

"We have four bodies but enough blood for twice that many," Pimdee said, looking back at the image of Jasper and Tama on the screen. "But I'm not one to create narratives until the facts are in."

Jenn thought the generators would be for emergencies like lights and refrigerators. So when electronic dance music burst from several speakers set up around the ballroom, she was surprised and cheered along with the others.

"Before the radios dropped out, they said the storm made landfall with 90 mile per hour winds," a DJ yelled into a microphone. "This isn't a storm party anymore. It's a hurricane party!"

There were more cheers.

The storm surge had long since flooded the beach. The dock and the patio restaurant were submerged. The ocean continued to rise, now at the second step from the top of the stairs leading up from the beach.

For Jenn, it felt like being on a ship at sea. The roiling ocean gave her a feeling of rocking back and forth though she was standing still. She expected the entire hotel to be lifted from its foundation and cast into the water at any second.

The thought made her shudder.

"Whoa!" exclaimed Tama.

She'd been coming up behind Jenn, her hands suspended in the air inches from Jenn's shoulders.

"I was about to grab you when you shivered," Tama said. "It was like your skin saw me coming. You think it's scared of me?"

Jenn mentally stammered as she struggled to locate a coy response.

"It shouldn't be," Tama said, giving Jenn a peck on the lips before wrapping her arms around her. "How incredible is this view?"

Jenn nodded as she turned back to the storm. She'd glimpsed Tama's pupils. They were almost as wide as her irises, making her eyes look black. She didn't know what drugs Tama was on, but imagined that's why she was handsy.

Not that she minded. Candice and Jasper hadn't stopped dancing since the music began. Candice was as awkward as Jenn in her flirting, but Jasper was one of the easiest going, most disarming people they'd met. Sure, within minutes of meeting him at a beach club in Goa, they knew he was a drug dealer, but he seemed downright apologetic about it. Like they'd discovered he was selling timeshares instead of MDMA.

"Have you ever been this close to a storm?" Tama asked, swaying behind Jenn as if dancing.

"Not like this," Jenn admitted. "You?"

"On land a couple of times but once at sea," Tama said. "We were going between Port Hedland, Australia and Bali in some old freighter when we hit a *huge* squall. It felt like we were in a carnival ride, only it went on for hours and hours instead of thirty seconds. They had these bunk belts on the beds to keep us from falling out, but I still slammed into the wall every few seconds. My entire left side was a bruise the next day."

"Ouch."

Tama nipped Jenn's left earlobe. With teeth.

"*Ouch*," Jenn repeated.

She stared at Tama's grinning reflection in the window as it overlaid the storm.

"Hey, I need to grab something from my room before it gets too dark in there," Jenn said. "Care to join?"

Tama grinned.

After dancing and drinking for hours, Candice hit a wall. She hadn't lost track of how many drinks she'd had—three rum-heavy Dark 'n' Stormys—but knew she hadn't balanced it well with water. Jasper, who didn't drink alcohol, was higher than the storm clouds. Unlike Tama, whom she'd seen getting extremely tactile with Jenn, ecstasy seemed to make Jasper disappear inward. He barely registered Candice's presence.

"You okay?" she asked finally, yelling over the now rave-style Bollywood music blasting from the speakers. When he didn't respond, she put her hand on his chest. He looked at her as if woken from a wonderful dream to a so-so reality.

"You okay?" he asked, clearly having not heard her question.

Candice had been on the fence about Jasper. Feeling dehydrated and tired didn't help, but she could've rallied. But looking into his glassy, drug-engorged eyes changed her mind.

"Getting a little tired. May head to the room for a nap."

"I, uh . . . think your friend went back to your room with my sister," Jasper said. "They've been gone a while."

Candice glanced over. Sure enough, Jenn and Tama were gone. They'd been on the road since summer with a month to go before having to return to Boston for the spring semester. In that time, Jenn had gotten crushes on two or three people only for them not to reciprocate. Candice didn't feel like intruding.

"I'll stay out here," Candice said. "I'll be fine."

"You can go to our room," Jasper suggested. "We've got two beds."

Candice raised an eyebrow. Jasper smiled.

"Just offering a bed! I'll let you into our room and scram. No problem. Cool?"

Candice opened her mouth to reply when the pungent smell of chemical cleaners hit her full in the face. She was instantly dizzy, the room spinning around her. She looked for the source of the scent even as her legs went out from under her. Jasper caught her before her head struck the floor.

"Are you all right?"

"What is that?" she asked. "That smell?"

Jasper looked around, then shook his head.

"I don't smell anything."

Candice closed her eyes, hoping it would pass, but the scent remained. It was strong. Overpowering. It came at her from all directions. At first, it felt like a poison. But now, something pleasant. Even delicious.

"I think you should lie down," Jasper said. "I'll just open the door and go."

"Oh, you can come in," Candice said, trying to nod, though her head moved in a circular motion. "If you try anything, I'll throw up on you."

"Deal," Jasper said, laughing. "Put your arm around my shoulder. We're just up the stairs."

"And that's the last time you saw either of them?" Attenberg asked.

"Yeah, they went up the stairs and disappeared," said Banjong Phutua, a sous chef at the resort who'd stepped in to bartend.

"Weren't you concerned about her state of inebriation?" Attenberg asked.

"It wasn't like that," Phutua said. "They seemed to be old friends. They talked about a restaurant they'd visited in India. Her friend had gone off with the other one and she needed looking after."

Sub-Lieutenant Pimdee reached for a cigarette for the fourth time, then remembered Attenberg's three previous requests he didn't smoke. He left the pack in his pocket. He'd already interviewed Phutua and knew his story by heart. He'd worried the chef's statement today might be different than the transcript Pimdee had already provided the FBI, but he'd been consistent.

"You never saw any of the four of them again?" Attenberg asked. "Did you see them the next morning, for instance?"

"I didn't see them, but I wasn't around," Phutua confirmed.

"Where were you?"

"The house where I and several other workers lived was swept away by a mudslide," he said. "I was recovering whatever belongings I could."

"Sorry to hear that," Attenberg said.

Pimdee was about to ask the two agents if they wanted to step out to discuss whether they had any more questions when his cell phone vibrated, indicating a text. After reading it, he held it out for Agent Attenberg to read, and then escorted them out of the interrogation room.

"It'll be another minute or two," he assured Phutua.

The text had been from Pimdee's office letting him know the report from Interpol on Jasper and Tama Bacevich, real names, Sergio Samaniego and Aurelia Idrovo had arrived. The email from Interpol was encrypted, requiring an IT worker to open it on their iPhone before printing off the station's printer. It was then put in a file folder on Pimdee's desk.

When Pimdee went to pick it up, however, Agent Rucker snatched it straight from his hands and flipped through it. Pimdee signaled the corporal waiting in the doorway.

"Corporal, please escort Agent Rucker out of my office, but not before returning that file to me."

Rucker glared at Pimdee, holding up the file.

"It says, 'human trafficking,'" Rucker shot back.

"Corporal?" Pimdee repeated.

"Wait outside, Jim," Attenberg ordered.

Rucker scowled, but did as he was told. Attenberg handed the file to Pimdee.

"I—" she began.

"No need to apologize," Pimdee replied, opening the file.

"I wasn't going to—"

"We're all on edge given the severity of the crime," Pimdee continued.

Attenberg fell silent. Pimdee read the report twice, then handed it to Attenberg.

"Jesus Christ," Attenberg said, reading quickly. "They were drug dealers, but also drug smugglers, and were even accused of manufacturing methamphetamine in Mozambique. Also, 'tik.' What's tik?"

"Methamphetamine," Pimdee said.

"They provided heroin to human traffickers and illegal brothels in at least four cities around the Indian Ocean," Attenberg said. "Drugs used to coerce and control, but also to hamper recall in case of arrest. Why weren't these people behind bars?"

"Excellent question," Pimdee said.

"So, maybe a kidnapping gone bad isn't far-fetched?"

"Possibly," Pimdee agreed. "But there was one more thing I asked Interpol about. On the last page."

Attenberg flipped there.

"A DNA profile of Samaniego and Idrovo?"

"Our forensics team has now identified eight unique individual blood samples taken from the room," Pimdee said. "Two were ID'd right away as belonging to Arevalo and Canoy. A third from Burton. Two more now from Samaniego and Idrovo."

"I'll assume the sixth is Jenn Schlosser but that leaves two more victims to be identified?"

"I wouldn't be so quick to say Schlosser is the sixth," Pimdee said.

"Why?"

"Because all eight of these samples were taken from inside her mouth."

Jasper's room was peaceful, silent and dark. Candice stared at the off-white ceiling from the bed, no longer minding the spinning of the room or the world beyond. The pungent odor had faded but hadn't gone away altogether. She could still smell it—*taste* it—in the air. It was unlike anything she'd smelled before, changing her perception like a drug. Inhaling it was like tasting something delicious every time she breathed. It was like chocolate. Fresh strawberries. Calla lilies.

Her late grandmother loved calla lilies. Even had a perfume that smelled like them. This scent took her right back to her grandmother's kitchen. The sensory memory was almost overpowering.

Jasper moved around the room, closing curtains and drawing a glass of water for Candice. When he handed her the glass, she realized the calla lily scent came from him.

"What is that?" she asked, dreamily.

"What's what?"

"The cologne you're wearing."

"I don't wear cologne," he said. "Maybe you're still smell—"

"No, it's on you," she said. "Come here."

He hesitated, but finally leaned over. Her nose filled with the scent, activating memories of childhood she hadn't remembered for years. It was like a mental time machine. There were other smells entwined with the calla lilies, taking her all through her life in vivid colors.

"This is incredible," she whispered.

He opened his mouth to reply and the scent increased tenfold. She moved her face to his, kissing him.

"You threatened to vomit on me if we did anything," he said, half-kissing her back.

"No. Only if *you* did anything."

She drank him in, enjoying the experience with her entire body. The scents that had only hung in the air a second before now cascaded through her body. It was as if she were reliving the endorphin rush of every wonderful moment of her entire life. The drug providing this had to be ferreted out from Jasper's body, where it hid in the recesses.

He bit her lip, barely enough to break the skin. As his saliva traveled over the exposed wound, Candice's vision blurred and her mind went white. It was as if she were being transformed into a new version of herself, one capable of consuming experience with—

"You bit me!" Jasper shrieked, jumping away and touching his tongue.

Blood poured over his bottom lip and ran down his chin and neck. Candice wasn't interested in the blood. She wanted what she'd tasted in his mouth. She rose. He backed away.

"Sorry," she said.

He softened. She struck him in the head with a lamp. His head hit the corner of a table with a crack as he crumpled to the floor.

Candice flew to his mouth, but there were new smells now. They came from the base of his skull. She pulled at the flesh atop his broken spinal column, but couldn't break it, even as her nose filled with the fragrant new scent. She bit at it with her teeth, but this was clumsy and took too long. She grew desperate.

Candice reached for the glass he'd used to bring her water. Breaking it against the table, she gripped a shard between two fingers and sliced through his skin. A thousand—no, *ten thousand*—flavors wafted into her nose.

It was exhilarating.

Jenn's right arm was broken in three places. Tama had fought back against her first attack using an ice bucket, but the drugs in her system slowed her down a half-step. This was the only advantage Jenn needed. She got her hands around Tama's neck and squeezed.

When Tama fell unconscious, Jenn thought she was dead. It was a surprise when blood spurted out of Tama's torso as Jenn tore into it, the motion indicative of a still beating heart. By the time Jenn opened Tama's throat, it had stopped.

She leaned back against the sofa, more in love with Tama than she'd ever been with anyone else in her life. The *ecstasy* the young woman had delivered to her! It was beyond words.

She wished Candice was there. At some point, she blacked out. When she awoke, Candice was beside her.

"Jenn?" Candice said, looking at the parts of Tama now strewn around the room.

"Oh," Jenn replied. "Oh, God. This is . . . I can explain. It's—"

"It's okay!" Candice said. "I can't explain it, but it's happening to me, too. I can . . . I can smell things."

"Me, too!" Jenn exclaimed. "It's like I can smell these entire worlds inside other people, worlds that connect with my own in wondrous ways. There's no past, no future—all present!"

"Exactly!" Candice agreed. "It began with smell—"

"Jasper?"

"Yeah, Jasper. But then . . . taste."

"Yeah, *taste!*" Jenn said, then shrank back. "But I can smell it in you, too. From all over."

Candice leaned toward Jenn. Inhaled. Salivated.

Jenn punched her with her shattered arm.

"No!" Jenn said, finding speech harder and harder. "We must keep one another safe. *Others.*"

"Yes, others," Candice echoed.

But the scents coming from within Candice were so powerful they almost overwhelmed Jenn's senses. She lunged for her friend. Candice batted her away.

"No!" Candice cried.

"I'm sorry!" Jenn said, tears in her eyes, though from pain or anguish at her own actions, she didn't know. "We have to protect ourselves from each other. We have to be smart."

"We can't share this," Candice said.

"No, we can't," Jenn agreed. "We have to be careful."

They consumed what they could of Tama before setting aside the parts they found unenticing. They tried to clean the room, but it was a lost cause. Worse, every time they neared the door or the wall, the aroma of the people nearest them wafted in. Jenn felt silly, like a cartoon character carried aloft by the visible scent lines of a pie.

She told Candice and they laughed about this for several minutes, jumping on the sofa. Jenn considered devouring Candice twice more, but was proud when she struck her head against the wall instead.

Jenn got the idea to shove towels under the doors to keep out the stench of others, but this only did so much. They'd need tape. No, *glue*. They'd need plastic sheets like shower curtains.

But their hunger overwhelmed them. They attacked each other again before they could head to the housekeeping pantry to steal supplies. Jenn took a bite out of Candice's ear. Candice bit off Jenn's right middle finger.

They stopped before things got out of hand, Jenn shoving a last piece of Tama's foot in her friend's mouth.

"We must be smart about this, remember?" Jenn said.

Candice nodded, then straightened.

"Jasper," she said, her voice a rasp.

They didn't bother cleaning Jasper's room. Besides, he'd conveniently fallen on a rug. They carried his body to the bathtub and rolled him in with a *thunk*, spending the next hour picking his bones clean. When done, they showered with their clothes on, bundled Jasper's remains in two backpacks, and carried them, the rug, and the shower curtain back to their room.

They were halfway down the fire stairs when Jenn noticed something.

"I can't smell you as well when you're under plastic," she said.

Candice set down the rug, soaked in blood and spinal fluid, to wrap the shower curtain around Jenn.

"You're right! I can still smell you a little bit, but maybe if we wrap it tighter?"

"Yeah," Jenn agreed. "Much tighter. We'll need more plastic."

"More plastic, more glue, more people," Candice replied.

The electricity didn't come on for another five hours. By then, Jenn and Candice were prepared. The resort's security officers

157

wouldn't force their door for another ninety-two hours.

Pimdee and the agents returned to the resort a final time. They'd spent two weeks chasing thin leads and rumors about human trafficking rings, but came up dry.

When the sub-lieutenant refused to add Arevalo and Canoy to his report as possible suspects, a frustrated Agent Attenberg had her superiors contact their counterparts in Manila to open an inquiry there. The FBI's suspicions were delivered to the Burton and Schlosser families and soon leaked to the press. For anyone following the case stateside, a salacious chronicle of two girls accidentally killed during a kidnapping gone wrong confirmed both their suspicions and worldview. They moved on.

"But you're not satisfied, are you?" Attenberg asked Pimdee, as they walked down the sandy beach.

The sub-lieutenant looked out over the water, shaking his head.

"There are still people unaccounted for, people you've decided don't matter," Pimdee said. "But my job is to make sure a crime like that doesn't happen again, not to provide a patched together story to grieving parents. I don't have the luxury of ignoring inconvenient evidence that doesn't prop up my narrative."

Attenberg ignored this remark, casting her gaze to the waterline.

"We've been out here four or five times," she said, nodding to a strange looking fish lying dead nearby. "Each time, there's some other crazy dead fish washed up here. How come?"

"The Indian Ocean is extraordinarily rich in its sea life," Pimdee said. "Unfortunately, some of its most fascinating species we only learn about after a tsunami or storm drags them up from the depths."

"Any of them good eating?" Agent Rucker snarked.

"Not that we've tried," Pimdee said, his annoyance with Rucker making him feel feverish. "While I can't say our fishermen don't occasionally prepare ones found in open water, those that wash up here are handed over to our marine biologists for study."

"You don't want to try one?" Rucker replied. "To see if you've discovered the new tuna or something?"

"No, some have been found to be filled with poisons or industrial toxins, others with rare parasitic bacteria," Pimdee said, shaking his head. "Did you know there are some fish down there, near the bottom, that feed on bacteria and other microorganisms?"

"Isn't that normal?"

"Not these," Pimdee said. "Bacteria enter the fish and it alters the way microbes in the digestive tract are balanced. The microbiome created by the bacteria tells the fish that instead of shrimp or plankton, it should eat the microorganisms the bacteria require to stay alive. So, it consumes and consumes, but only the bacteria get fed. Soon, the fish dies and the bacteria seek another host."

"Disturbing," Attenberg said.

"If you're a fish, I suppose," Pimdee replied, staring out at the water. "If you're a fish."

GOOD TIME IN THE BAD LANDS

Laura Keating

MARCY WAS SPRAWLED ACROSS THE backseat, sucking on a melting chocolate bar as Aaron screamed, "My side! My side! Stay off my side!" He shoved her thick leg with his sticky hands.

The car was hot. The a/c was dead. The parched wind pummeling the car's occupants smelled like mud. Bub, the family's unfixed golden retriever, hopped from the front seat to the backseat, drool flying off his red tongue, and barking his head off. The dog's huge tail whacked Lenora Parker, sitting in the front seat, right in the face. Dog hair stuck to her lip-gloss.

"Aaron, stop it," said the kids' mother. "You're making the dog crazy."

"It's her!"

"I'm not doing anything," said Marcy innocently, smearing her Mars bar around her mouth to lick off later. "I'm not even touching him." She pressed her toe harder on the clip of Aaron's seatbelt, clamping him tighter. Aaron shrieked.

"Would you kids shut up?" their father growled, hunched over the steering wheel, glasses slipping perilously to the tip of his nose.

"I'm just cooling off."

"My side!"

"Shut up! Shut up or I'll stop this car!" bellowed their father, Mike Parker. A vein in his temple throbbed. "Lifted Jesus on a stick, I will stop this car!"

But they knew he never would. They were making good time.

Every July, the family went to visit Mike's parents in Moose Jaw. The trip from Prince Albert never seemed long, in theory. Three hours and forty minutes, the internet would have you believe. With their iPad charged, the little monsters could even stay occupied for an hour or two. The rest of the time they whined, but even that could be broken up with a quick pit stop at a Burger King or, better still, a McDonald's. Usually the hardest part of the drive was just keeping awake; even in the daytime, the flat, unbending prairie landscape had a way of sucking you in.

It must have been a kind of madness to leave the electronics at home this time, Mike figured, as his twelve-year-old daughter kicked the back of his seat for the hundredth time. The other day he had looked at his kids (his youngest already eight) and realized he could not distinguish one single summer vacation from the other. It was all the same and mostly a blur, just like the yellow canola fields and big blue sky they passed but never really looked at every summer. Didn't they want to do something special? Marcy was already looking at boys and kissing her poster of Harry Styles before bed every night. Next year she'd be a teenager. She might get a job busing tables; she might not even want to go on family vacation anymore and would have the excuse of work to lay on him.

Then it struck him. They'd never been to the Badlands. A natural wonder practically in their backyard, and in all these years they'd never been. He warmed to the idea, already basking in the nostalgia his kids would one day pour on him like a sweet balm in his old age: stories about the great time they had that one year, that last year before the real world came flooding in and swept them away into the lifelong routines of work and responsibility.

He decided they would leave extra early, see the sights at Big Muddy, and then spend a night in a motel. Len had protested; if they were going to stay somewhere, it should be a hotel. But he wasn't made of money and he was already burning the extra gas to make this trip special.

He told the kids not to pack their electronics, they were going to have good, old-fashioned fun.

The protests had been swift and severe.

"Nothing old-fashioned is good," insisted Marcy. "If it were good, it would be the now-fashioned."

"We're going to see the sights, Marce," said Mike. "Take it in. No filters."

"That's not fair! Lots of grass, old rocks, and road. Big whoop."

"If you paid attention, you might find it's a very nice whoop," said Mike. "You'll look back on these trips one day. Best days of your life."

"Kill me now," said Marcy, flopping back onto her bed.

Aaron took it a little better, but his eyes teared up when he was told he couldn't bring the family laptop to watch movies, either.

"I'll be so bored," he said, turning on the waterworks. Silent tears slipped down his ruddy cheeks. "And so will Marcy."

"Are you crying?" said Mike, not sure if it was good parenting to laugh at his kid. But he was so tired, had been for twelve years. Confused laughter was forever on a knife's edge with a parent.

"I don't want to go to the Bad Man's, I just want to go to grandma's."

"We're still going to grandma's, just after the Bad*lands*."

Aaron tipped his head back like Charlie Brown and started to howl, revving up to a good bawl. Mike backed out of the room and shut the door.

They were nearing Moose Jaw. Soon they would be in unfamiliar territory. Mike leaned across the gearshift, one eye peeking over the grimy dashboard, and slapped the glove compartment until it flopped open.

"Hey, honey. Dig out the map and get me some directions, will ya?"

"I can't. We left our phones," moaned Len, head back and eyes closed as she fanned her face with an expired Subway coupon book.

"Paper maps, honey, we have paper maps."

With one eye over the dash and one hand steady on the wheel, Mike shuffled through old take-out napkins, a waterlogged car manual, and a lifetime worth of dead air fresheners. His hand landed on a crusty sheaf of pages torn from an atlas found at a yard sale years ago. He tossed the papers to Len's lap and sat back up. The blood rushing to his head made him see silver spots.

Len sipped from the jumbo Gatorade bottle she'd had safely nestled between her knees. It wasn't Gatorade. Without opening her eyes, she held the pages backwards over the console. Bub, lying on

162

the middle seat, tried to lick her wrist.

"Marce, read the maps for Daddy."

"Can I have a dollar?"

"You can have a dollar."

"Five dollars."

"Marce, read the maps," said Mike, "or we give Aaron the dollar."

"I want a dollar," whined Aaron.

"You got to work for money," said Marcy, snatching the pages. "And I wouldn't hire you for a million bucks." Aaron started to cry.

"Marce," said Len. "Hire your brother."

"Five bucks."

"Five, if you hire your brother and pay him."

Marcy shoved the papers at Aaron.

"One dollar. No benefits," said Marcy, and Aaron started to read the maps out loud, happy to be making a wage. Marcy lounged back again and licked her lips; there wasn't anything good you could get with four dollars.

They had to stop for gas. Aaron had gotten them turned around (somehow), but it wasn't long before he realized his mistake. Still, Mike was angry.

"We were making good time," he muttered as the kids bolted from the car, heading straight to the last unoccupied picnic table beside the gas station restaurant. They clambered on top and took turns leaping as far off as they could.

Len slipped on her sunglasses and broad hat as she cradled her bottle under one thin arm. Bub barked at them from the back seat. Len cringed at the light.

"God it's so hot. How can a place that gets so cold get so hot?" She was from Victoria. She missed the unsurprising climate.

Mike began digging through the trunk. "Place this flat, it's like a clean slate; the weather can be as extreme as it wants."

"I don't think that's right."

He found the cooler at the very back, after taking out their assorted luggage and the plastic bags for extra shoes. He handed out sandwiches at the table: peanut butter and banana for Aaron, cheese for Marcy, cucumber and ham for Len and him. They leashed Bub to the leg of the table and filled his water dish from the gallon jug they'd packed.

Mike smiled around at his family as they quietly ate their

sandwiches and watched the other travelers. His heart swelled with pride. This was it. This was the stuff of memory, of Norman Rockwell, of Americana. Wrong country, but same idea: The Great Family Car Trip. He'd brought his old digital camera and now was the perfect time for a picture. He'd even print this one out, display it somewhere they would always look at it and remember the good times. He got up wordlessly (he didn't want to spook the moment) and headed back to the car.

A huge SUV had pulled up beside their car. It was dark blue and, despite the dusty summer roads, was so clean Mike could see himself in its doors like a warped mirror. Two little girls in matching unicorn t-shirts hopped out of the back doors. A young woman in cute yoga pants followed suit from the passenger seat. The girls stretched as their father opened his door. It banged into Mike's passenger-side door. The young father saw Mike, and then carefully stepped out of his car. He straightened his polo shirt as Mike stood by.

"Hey, this your car? Don't think it left a mark." He noticed there were scratches all down the doors, from mirror to taillight.

"No, I'm over . . . over there." Mike pointed vaguely off across the lot. The two girls and their mother were heading to the restaurant. "Family trip?"

"We just got back from Castle Butte," said the young man, not moving from his car. He hit the key fob and his doors chirped locked.

"We're on our way there, too," said Mike proudly. But the SUV man shook his head. He slipped on a pair of Ray-Bans and dropped his keys into the pocket of his shorts.

"Weather's supposed to change. This might be a bad time to be getting there."

"We got turned around coming down here," said Mike, as though this might help things. "Son couldn't read a map."

"From here it's a straight shot, more or less. But there's a shortcut," he added. "If you go back about five kilometers—it seems counterintuitive, I know—but in the end it'll cut off about thirty minutes of drive time."

"We know where we're going." Mike had not liked the defensive tone that had crept into his voice. Neither did the young man. He turned his back to Mike and began to walk around his vehicle.

"Just saying, the window of opportunity might be closing for today."

"We're just heading out."

"Okay." And the young father strolled off to meet his girls who were quietly waiting under the restaurant portico. Mike stood looking after him, the sun beating on his balding head.

"Let's go, let's go," he told his family, back at the picnic table. "Time's wasting."

"We just sat down," said Len.

"You can sit in the car."

The kids were chasing each other. Aaron had Bub running with him. The dog spotted a ground squirrel and bolted, jerking the boy to the ground and dragging him over the dusty grass. Aaron dropped the leash. Bub got the squirrel and bit it in half, happily flinging half away as he chomped up the butt-end and ran to Mike to show off his prize. Aaron got to his feet. He was covered from neck to knees in big, ugly grass stains. He began to scream. Marcy tackled the dog, shouting, "I got the sonovabitch!"

"Marce!" said Len.

"He is!"

"Let's go!" shouted Mike. Half of the picnickers were watching the show now. He grabbed Bub by the collar and, hunched over, began to drag him away before he remembered the leash. "In the car, now."

Aaron cried that he hadn't eaten his apple yet.

Mike tied the dog to the table and threw half-eaten sandwiches and bent paper plates into the cooler. He dumped the rest of the water on Bub's snout to wash the squirrel off. At the car, he somehow managed to get the dog in the back and everything in the trunk in less than five minutes. The kids took another ten. Len sat in the passenger seat, her head back and eyes closed. Aaron refused to get in the car if Bub was still there, on account of him ruining his favorite Batman t-shirt.

"For Christ's sake, he's a dog! He didn't know," said Mike. "You were the one running him."

"It's completely your fault," agreed Marce.

"Marcy, get inside."

"Bub's all wet."

"Kids, get in the car. Mommy's melting!" moaned Len.

Mike saw the SUV man coming out of the restaurant. His daughters stood at his side like obedient shadows. Mike flung open the door and picked his wailing boy up by collar and waistband and tossed him inside. Marcy, with Aaron between her and the dog, jumped in after.

The stench of hot rubber lay in their wake as Mike put the pedal to the metal and they fishtailed on the dusty asphalt back onto the highway.

The car was hotter than ever. The unrolled windows were no help. Aaron wouldn't stop crying. He had worked himself up and was hiccupping uncontrollably, maintaining a whine like a pierced balloon. Every time he began to calm down, Marcy would gnash her teeth at him, re-enacting Bub's exuberant kill, and get him started again. Len, unable to cope with the heat and noise, pounded back the rest of her bottle in three open-neck chugs and passed out, cheek stuck to her seatbelt, only rousing long enough to groan, "Too hot."

Mike could see thunderheads in the distance. The park would be closed off if it started to rain, and then what? Without taking his eyes off the road, he bunched the atlas pages together in his fist and thrust them at Aaron like a trash bouquet.

"Find a shortcut, Aer."

"He'll just mess it up," said Marcy.

"Daddy needs a shortcut!"

"Ten bucks."

"I'll stop this car, I swear to god!"

Marcy grabbed the pages and Mike, eyes dead ahead, was never sure if she did it on purpose. But the second she had them, Marcy let out a big, cartoonish, "Oh, no!"

The map pages fluttered around the cab like panicked birds. Before Mike could shout at her to get them back together, they were sucked out the back windows and sent tumbling in the tailwind of the car. Even Marcy looked shocked at how fast it'd happened.

Mike's stream of obscenities was incoherent. All he'd wanted was a good time, to give his kids a trip to remember. Was that too much to ask? He was sure *he'd* remember this trip; only a river of vodka could wash this one away. He took a breath. A species of laugh that was not entirely healthy escaped his lips. The kids quieted at once. In the stillness, he heard a flapping. A single page had gotten stuck to the sticky console between the seat and the cupholders. He grabbed it, his head nodding down and then up as he tried to read the topographical features and keep his eyes on the road. A horn blared as he crossed the median and he swerved out of the way.

A grin pressed his lips back. The page was more worn than the others had been, like it had come from a different atlas. But the map was just what he needed. Up ahead, there'd be a turnoff; it'd take them right to where they wanted to go. They'd make up for their pit stop and then some. Why hadn't he just looked at the maps himself from the start? Old-fashioned maps, they never let you down!

No sooner had he read the directions than did the turnoff appear. A crusty wooden signpost no higher than a mailbox with faded, white letters spelling out BAD LANDS materialized so fast he almost asked if the others saw it, too. Mike hit the brakes and cut hard to the right. The skidding car kicked up a plume of dust and rocks. The kids were thrown into one another; Bub hit the floor and yelped; Len jolted awake and grabbed her door handle, skinning her knuckles.

The new road was not as well-maintained as the main road, but it was empty. Mike could see some hills in the distance, and he laughed again. This road probably gave some of the best views. Locals probably knew all about this road but kept it to themselves.

The smile had become plastered on Mike's face. Not a single car behind them or in front; it was clear driving. Even the clouds didn't look so dark; everything was a little bit brighter. He pressed harder on the gas. Things were going to be fine.

"This doesn't look right," said Marcy after half an hour. The landscape was changing. The grass was greener and longer. The bare patches were hard and sharp, with huge juts of rock stabbing out of the ground at odd angles like stone knives. "We should turn back."

"No, Marcy," said Mike, grin fixed on his face. "We're making great time."

More rocks joined the sharp outcrops. Aaron thought they looked like the giant termite hills he'd seen on a nature show. Vines twisted up some of the rocks; flowers with huge, waxy leaves and enormous purple and yellow heads swayed between others.

"Michael," said Len softly. The sky had taken on an interesting shade of pink. Small green clouds roiled above them, rubbing across the sky like enormous snail trails. The plant life on the sides of the road began to stretch and writhe.

Aaron began to cry, "Daddy, go back!" as Marcy put on a high, mocking voice, "Go back! Whine, whine, whine. That's you. You just whine, whine, whine, whine!" she laughed, and Len began to fan herself again, "It's too hot. Kids, please. I can't take it."

A huge, dark shadow passed over the car. Marcy began to giggle, a weird and guttural chortling. Aaron shrieked louder, "Go back!"

The air shimmered like warped glass. A smell like burning hair began to fill the car. Aaron rolled up his window, but the others stayed open. The overgrowth in the ditches whipped lightly at the car doors and created a syncopated, metal drumming.

Something darted in front of the car. Mike hit it dead on, thumping over the body, but they'd all seen it: a ground squirrel the size of a pit bull with teeth like knitting needles jutting out of its fleshy, pink mouth. The abomination got caught up under the car, bouncing the vehicle as it pounded along. Mike swerved to shake it loose, leaving a bloody trail for fifty meters before it was dislodged. Marcy laughed and beat on the back window. Aaron's crying shrieks reached an almost soundless high.

"I can't take it," muttered Len, as the kids giggled and screamed, sinking deeper into her chair. "I can't."

The huge shadow passed by again. The whole car jolted. Mike glanced up. Massive claws punctured the roof with a crinkling grind of metal. The windshield exploded as the roof peeled back like a sardine can. The huge creature lifted upwards with two powerful beats of its leathery wings, dropping the scrap roof on the road behind them. The creature swooped low and shot past. Mike saw it had no face—just one huge, black eye.

"How does it eat!" shouted Marcy, laughing more steadily. She threw her arms around Mike's seat and chest. Her forearms appeared greenish in the light, mottled with tiny, yellow warts.

"Daddy's trying to drive," he told her. There was a great ripping sound and half his headrest was bitten off.

The giant bat reeled around, coming back.

"Make dad turn around!" Aaron screamed, beating on his mother's seat.

"I can't," Len muttered, over and over. "I can't, I can't . . ."

"We're almost there, Aer-bear!" Mike cheered. The wind rushed through his hair, tossed his glasses aside and out of the car. He didn't need them; he could see just fine. "Just a little further!"

The bat sailed over and, without losing a beat, grabbed Aaron. Within seconds, his screams were too distant to be heard.

"Wow!" said Mike. "Can that thing move!"

Marcy whirled around, jumped on her seat, and gibbered excitedly. She was no longer making words. Knots bulged up her spine and she dug at the seat with her clawed feet. Bub barked, scrambling to get into the front. Marcy caught the dog's tail with her teeth. Blood slashed across the seat. With a frantic, almost human yelp, the dog leapt from the moving car and bolted into the ever-growing under-brush. Marcy screeched, vaulted from the car, and gave delighted chase.

"Don't worry about the dog, honey," Mike assured Len, his grin reaching all the way to his ears. "Marce'll get him."

"I can't," Len repeated. The words were flabby and sluggish. Her lips had become an upside-down U; the skin of her face stuck to her chin and her chest, as she slowly puddled into the seat. She melted to the floor in glossy, reeking tendrils.

"That's okay, honey!" But when he looked over, she had already slipped out the crack at the bottom of her door. That was okay, too. Less weight in the car, faster on the road! Mike pressed down on the gas. The tailpipe dragged and sparked; licks of flame shot out the exhaust.

His eyes grew huge and excited as the wind whipped his hair around. Nothing like a good, old-fashioned road trip. He could see something ahead. The end of the road, maybe, or perhaps something bigger. He couldn't tell. It didn't matter.

He was making really great time.

ACKNOWLEDGMENT FROM THE EDITOR

Thank you to author and Grindhouse Press owner, C.V. Hunt, for believing in and providing a home for this anthology.

BIOS

Sadie Hartmann
Foreword

Sadie Hartmann lives in the Pacific Northwest with her husband, their big children, and a French Bulldog. She reviews horror fiction for *Cemetery Dance Online* and *SCREAM Magazine*. You can find her articles and interviews at *LitReactor.com*, *Tor Nightfire*, and *FANGO-RIA*. She is the co-owner of a monthly horror book subscription service called Night Worms. Reading, reviewing, and promoting horror fiction is a lifestyle she plans on maintaining forever—even from beyond the grave.

S.E. Howard
"You've Been Saved"

S.E. Howard grew up in the heart of the Bluegrass, and has worked as a newspaper reporter, travel writer, and magazine editor. She's written about some of Kentucky's most infamous haunts, including Liberty Hall, Bobby Mackie's Music World, and Waverly Hills Sanitorium. When she's not writing, she enjoys genealogy and learning more about local history. Her family traces back to frontier statesman William Whitley, who built the first brick house west of the Allegheny Mountains, and introduced counter-clockwise horse racing to the United States. A registered nurse, she is also a Certified Specialist in Poison Information. Find out more at www.sehoward.com.

Greg Sisco
"Summers with Annie"

Greg Sisco is the author of six dark fiction novels. In 2019, he was featured on Austin Film Festival's annual list of 25 Screenwriters to Watch. His love of movies could be described as creepy.

Asher Ellis
"Expertise"

Asher Ellis is a screenwriter, educator, and author of the novels *The

Remedy, PET, and *Curse of the Pigman.* He has written multiple award-winning short films, including *My Name Is Art,* which was part of Amazon's first annual "All Voices Film Festival." When not working on his latest project, Asher teaches at several colleges throughout New Hampshire and in his home state of Vermont. Visit him at www.asherellis.com.

Hailey Piper
"Unkindly Girls"

Hailey Piper is the author of *Benny Rose, the Cannibal King* and *The Possession of Natalie Glasgow.* She is a member of the HWA, and her short fiction appears in *Year's Best Hardcore Horror, Daily Science Fiction, The Arcanist,* and elsewhere. She lives with her wife in Maryland, where she haunts their apartment making spooky noises. Find her on Twitter via @HaileyPiperSays or at www.haileypiper.com.

Waylon Jordan
"Deep in the Heart"

Waylon Jordan is a longtime horror fan who fell in love with the macabre when he was a kid and never grew out of it. In the last few years, he has established a name for himself in the field of online horror journalism and as an advocate for LGBTQ representation in the genre space.

Kenzie Jennings
"Peelings"

Kenzie Jennings is an English professor living in the sweltering tourist hub of Central Florida. She is the author of the cannibal wedding novel, *Reception,* and the upcoming splatter western, *Red Station* (Death's Head Press). Her short horror fiction has appeared in *Dig Two Graves, Vol. 1* and *Deep Fried Horror: Mother's Day Edition.*

Malcolm Mills
"The Difference Between Crocodiles and Alligators"

Malcolm Mills is a NYC actor, filmmaker, and horror-soundtrack composer. He's proudly played necromancers, stalkers, vampires, psycho mothers, mad scientists, faery kings, and cult leaders on stage and screen. "You were creepy" has been the most common feedback.

V. Castro
"The Cucuy of Cancun"

V. Castro is a Mexican American writer originally from Texas and now residing in the UK. When not caring for her three children, she dedicates her time to writing. For more information about her books and other publications, please visit www.vvcastro.com. She can also be followed on Twitter and Instagram at @vlatinalondon.

Jeremy Herbert
"Family Taylor Vacation '93"

Jeremy Herbert is a fan of frozen beverages, loud shirts, and drive-in movies. He makes award-winning horror shorts for the price of minor kitchen appliances and writes crime for outlets like *Ellery Queen* and *Mystery Tribune*. He owes his passion for theme parks to home videos a lot like the one in his story.

Scott Cole
"The Penanggalan"

Scott Cole is a writer, artist, and graphic designer living in Philadelphia. He likes old radio dramas, old horror comics, weird movies, cold weather, coffee, and a few other things, too. Find him on social media, or at 13visions.com.

Chad Stroup
"Sex with Dolphins"

Stroup is the author of the novels, *Secrets of the Weird* (Grey Matter Press), *Sexy Leper* (Bizarro Pulp Press), and the comic series, *Hag* (American Gothic Press). He has published several short stories in magazines and anthologies, such as *Shock Totem*, *Forbidden Futures*, *Chiral Mad 4*, *Lost Films*, and *Splatterlands*, and his dark poetry has appeared in all volumes of the HWA Poetry Showcase. Follow him on Instagram or Twitter at @chadxstroup.

Patrick Lacey
"Caught a Glimpse"

Patrick Lacey spends his nights and weekends writing about things that make the general public uncomfortable. He lives in Massachusetts with his wife, his daughter, his oversized cat, and his muse, who is likely trying to kill him. Follow him on Twitter at @patlacey.

Mark Wheaton
"In the Water"

Mark Wheaton is a novelist (*Emily Eternal* and, forthcoming, *The Quake Cities*), and screenwriter (*Friday the 13th*, *The Messengers*) living in Los Angeles.

Laura Keating
"Good Time in the Bad Lands"

Laura Keating is a writer of thrillers, horror, and speculative fiction. Her work has been published in several anthologies. Originally from St. Andrews, New Brunswick, she now lives in Montréal, Québec, where—when not working on a novel—she works as a freelance writer and editor. You can follow her on Twitter at @LoreKeating, or find more about her work on her website, www.lorekeating.com

Samantha Kolesnik
Editor

Samantha Kolesnik is an award-winning writer and film director living in central Pennsylvania. Her screenplays and short films have been recognized at top genre film festivals and her fiction has appeared in notable literary magazines including *The Bitter Oleander*, *The William and Mary Review*, and *Barnstorm*. Her debut novel, *True Crime*, was released by Grindhouse Press in early 2020.

Other Grindhouse Press Titles

Printed in Great Britain
by Amazon